SUGAR AIN'T SO SWEET

BOOK 1 OF THE EVERYTHING NICE SERIES

NALEIGHNA KAI
LA AMMITAI

MACRO PUBLISHING GROUP

Macro Publishing Group

Macro Marketing & Promotions Group

Cover designed by: Woodson Creative Studio

Interior design by: Macro Marketing & Promotions Group

EBOOK ISBN: 9781952871504

LA AMMITAI
I dedicate this book in loving memory of my:
Son, Kylon Greenwood
(July 2009 – Dec. 2009)
Father, William L. Greenwood Jr.
(Sept. 1965 – July 2018)
**You are my greatest inspiration to live life intentionally and
purposefully.**
I will always love you.

NALEIGHNA KAI
To my writing tribe, you inspire me ... always.
*To my son ... I love you so much and I'm grateful that you've been the best
part of my life.*

ACKNOWLEDGMENTS

Special thanks goes out to: The Creator from whom all Blessings and opportunities flow, Sandy (my true mother), my son, J. L. Woodson (for the awesome cover designs for this Merry Hearts series), Sesvalah, Bettye Odom, Janice M. Allen, Debra J. Mitchell, Royce Slade Morton, Bunny Ervin, J. L. Campbell, Kelly Peterson, Janine A. Ingram, Ehryck F. Gilmore, Betty Clawson, Jamyi Joy, Stephanie M. Freeman, Unique Hiram, Marie L. McKenzie, Shawn Williams, Dr. Vanessa Howard, the Kings of the Castle Ambassadors, Members of Naleighna Kai's Literary Cafe, the members of NK's Tribe Called Success, the members of Namakir Tribe, and to you, my dear readers . . . thank you all for your support.

Much love, peace, and joy,
Naleighna Kai

ACKNOWLEDGEMENTS FROM LA AMMITAI

All praise goes to God. Thank you for presenting me with opportunity after opportunity to do more of what I love—creating and writing. Lord, thank you for leading me to the right places and giving me the right support. I'm thankful for the talents you have trusted me with the gift to others.

I give flowers to my significant other, Ken Woods, for his unwavering support with this project. You've been one of my biggest supporters and always the first to share any of my content. Thank you for exercising understanding and compassion through the long hours and late nights I've spent tapping into my purpose. I'm grateful for your attentiveness to my needs when I'm in a creative zone. Your acts of service and attention to detail never go unnoticed. I love you.

I give flowers to my literary agent and writing coach, Naleighna Kai, for not only spear-heading this project, but for also being an amazing teacher on my literary journey. Five years ago, who knew that I would be co-authoring books with a USA Today and Essence® Bestselling Author? Naleighna, thank you for your knowledge and wisdom. I'm grateful to you for always selflessly putting the tribe before yourself. You're truly one of the most noble people I've ever met.

I give flowers to my literary tribe, NK Tribe Called Success (also known as Cavalcade of Authors), a collective of National, Award-winning, and #1 Bestselling Authors. Thank you for all your help, support, and love. I give extra flowers to Stephanie, U.M., and Martha, for holding me accountable with writing sprints—helping me reach the finish line once again. There's no vibe like my tribe's vibe.

I give flowers to my family and friends for their continuous support. My mother, Jacquelyn Greenwood, is another superfan. Thank you, mom, for always believing in me and encouraging me to do what God has planned for me to do. To my children, Cameron and D'Angelo, I love you both so much. You boys have been so graceful and flexible with me in this busy chapter of my life. Just know that God is working through me and all around me. It is my hope that I'm setting the stage for you to allow him to do the same in your lives.

Last, but not least, I give flowers to all my followers, readers, supporters, and newcomers. If you've read any of my previous works, you know that personal development is my jam. This time we're going to switch it up a little. Debuting in the genre of romantic fiction was different, yet fun. I hope you all thoroughly enjoy this short story just as much as I enjoyed co-writing it.

CHAPTER 1

I will die if I stay here ...

Shannan's entire family sat at the dinner table enjoying a meal which took her three hours to prepare, while she mowed the jungle of their front yard, seething the entire time. She stopped to empty the bag but froze when her mother-in-law's voice carried from the open pantry window, "I had to fake a damn heart attack to make this stupid heifer get with the program."

Faked a heart attack? Wait. What?

Monique Hallerin had faked that entire one-month ordeal so Shannan would take over the daunting task of shopping, preparing, cooking, then serving Sunday dinners for fifteen people every week, only for her to criticize nearly everything that Shannan did. Faked it so Shannan's husband, Zach, would pick up the slack on her bills. All while her brothers-in-law and most of her children parked their lazy behinds at the dining room table every Sunday and didn't lift a finger to help. Shannan was way past tired—exhausted was a better word.

"Guests don't wash dishes," her husband said when she mentioned they could pitch in with clean up. Well, to be honest, neither did he and he hadn't been a guest since they'd said, "I do."

What she should've said on the day they were married, fifteen years ago, was, "I don't," then ran past his overbearing mother and four shiftless brothers, then out the church doors to freedom.

"I had to fake a damn heart attack to make this stupid heifer get with the program."

Shannan, who had seven children of her own, was now responsible for duties that her mother-in-law had done for most of her non-married life; catering to those grown ass men sitting at her dining room table at this very moment while Shannan was outside doing something she had first asked her husband, then one of them, to do.

Rage hit Shannan full force.

She staggered away from the mower, rushed into the house, ran up the stairs and snatched up her tote. She halted at the threshold of her bedroom for a moment, extracting the small shoebox in the back of the closet. A set of credit cards, passport, birth certificate, social security card, and all the hidden cash found its way into the tote. She glanced at the summer wardrobe spilling over onto Zach's side and decided there wasn't anything she wanted to take. She tipped down the rear stairway into the kitchen, snatched the keys from a hook near the door to put as much distance between herself and those people as possible.

Shannan only vaguely heard the youngest of her seven children call her name. Her heart constricted as she ignored them, tears blinding her as she slid behind the wheel of an SUV that was almost a second home. Basketball. Volleyball. Football. Gymnastics. PTA. Never any breaks between or any time for her to simply breathe.

I will die if I stay here.

Those seven words came to mind, summarizing her current status. Something that first hit her when she had the argument with Zach before his family arrived ...

"No, my brothers shouldn't have to wash a dish in my house," Zachary had *protested without bothering to look up from the current prosthetics project spread out over the basement. "My mother spent a week in the hospital and*

she can't handle it anymore. This dinner is how we stay close. I don't see what the problem is."

"The problem is, that it's all too much," she replied, putting aside her own work on the latest puzzle she was creating for the daily newspaper to focus more on the conversation that was long overdue. "I'm beginning to dread Sundays. I don't have any day of rest."

"Well, if you gave up that job you've been playing at, then you wouldn't be so tired all the time," he quipped.

"I shouldn't have to give up anything," she shot back. He'd always considered the six figures she made from being a Master Cruciverbalist—crossword puzzle creator—frivolous. His career as a prosthetist brought in just under what she did. There had been a bone of contention on that score.

"Then it looks like you're going to be busy." Zachary shrugged. "You'll be alright."

"Wouldn't have to be so busy if you and the boys helped around here," she countered.

"My mother raised five boys on her own and never complained," he said, keeping his focus on the circuitry in his hands.

"And she was on her own because she ran your father off," she replied. "Let's be real about that."

Zachary's face twisted into a mask of annoyance as he glared at her. "I can't talk about this with you."

"I'm done talking. I'm tired," she snapped. "There's going to come a time when I say to hell with it."

Zach paused at the end of the wooden bench, scoffing as he asked, "And where are you going to go? Who's going to be a father to seven children?"

"They have a father," she said, and the sorrow of her reality was heavy indeed. "I need a husband."

THE MOMENT SHANNAN hit the expressway, she wiped her tears with the back of a trembling hand. Then she nearly crashed the car as a startling thought hit her.

I cannot leave my baby girl in that house.

CHAPTER 2

Shannan popped a U-turn and headed back home. "Call London."

The car's hands-free connection put her on the line with her baby girl. "Sweetheart, step out of the dining room so you can hear me."

"Yes ma'am," London said, though she could barely be heard over the usual debate going on with Zach and his brothers.

"Listen to me well," Shannan said, pushing the car to right above the posted speed limit. "In five minutes, get Kriss, walk out of the back door and—"

"Mom, what's going on?"

"In five minutes," Shannan repeated in a sterner tone. "Get Kriss and both of you walk out of the back door and meet me in the drive-way. Do *not* tell anyone."

"Mom?"

"Do you understand me?"

"Yes ma'am," she whispered.

"I'll be there soon."

* * *

Twenty-three minutes later, Shannan sat on the chaise part of a micro suede sectional across from her mother, Jackie, a feisty woman with cinnamon-kissed skin and short curly hair. A woman who had been banished from the family home by Shannan's Irish father when he, a wealthy oil magnate, demanded that she serve up some of his rich friends in the same way he was able to sample their wives.

Jackie left that night taking Shannan and her twin, heading back home to Atlanta to heal her wounds. Unfortunately, that wasn't the only hurt he would inflict. The ugly court battle cost Jackie hundreds of thousands only to have the Chicago courts side with her ex-husband, his money and power.

She lost all rights to her girls, and Ernest Breckenridge did everything in his power to eliminate Jackie from their lives. When Shannan turned twelve, she sought her mother out and established a secret relationship with the woman who was never far from her heart and mind. Her twin, Megan, did not feel the same.

As London and Kriss took in a movie in one of the upstairs bedrooms, Jackie listened closely to Shannan's issues with the marriage, without commenting, as Shannan explained she was done.

"I always wanted your happiness," Jackie admitted, grabbing a shot glass and a bottle of Fireball from the liquor cabinet. "Regardless of what you thought."

"You never liked him."

"I liked him before you got married. After that, I tolerated him for your sake," she admitted, holding up a second shot glass and quirking a brow when Shannan shook her head to decline. "And I don't have to like him. I'm not the one who's married to him. I voiced my concern early on."

"One time."

"That should've been enough," she said, taking a sip and grimacing. "I said from day one that his family's influence would be much too strong for a happy marriage. That you should move to another city when that opportunity came, and you would've had a chance."

"I listened," Shannan whispered. "But evidently I didn't hear you."

Jackie placed a hand over Shannan's. "You were determined to have him, no matter what I observed. He wasn't like that in the beginning, but with the unnecessary input from that wench and those hooligans, he became selfish from the moment you walked down the aisle. Every time you let him chip away at anything you wanted, you became more a part of him and less of you." Her dark brown eyes scanned Shannan from head to toe. "Evidently, it kept going until there were no more of you to give. It's been painful to watch you sacrifice so much and receive so little; all because you believe that your entire life should be wrapped up in him, trying to prove something you didn't need to prove—that you were Black enough despite your pale skin. Black school. Black man. Black children. All as a way to reconnect with that part of me that was missing all those years."

While trying to process that hard truth, Shannan extracted her mother's glass from her hands.

Jackie lightly slapped Shannan's fingers. "Hey, get your own," she teased as she reclaimed her drink.

Instead, Shannan swiped the bottle and took a swig straight from the source.

"You used everything in your power to make him happy, despite the fact that he stopped putting forth the effort to make *you* happy." Jackie slid the bottle out of Shannan's reach. "When a man's mother has that much of a hold on him, it's a battle to get her to loosen up. And that wench has a Kung Fu grip. She never wanted to let go, and the truth be told, he never wanted her to let go."

Jackie reached out for Shannan, who willingly went into her arms. She laid her head on her mother's shoulder. "I love my grandchildren, but I know the reason they're here and it isn't because they were wanted," Jackie sincerely stated. "You only wanted two children, regardless of gender. You had five more because he demanded you keep going until he had that girl child he demanded. So now there are five additional casualties of this marriage."

She paused, then asked. "Does he know how successful your editing business has become?"

"No."

"Thank God for that," she said, easing off the sofa and stretching. "And you put that money in your private account, as I suggested?"

"Yes, ma'am. Some of it's in emergency cash. I'm holding it right now."

"See, I raised you right." Jackie lifted her glass in salute. "How long are you going to stay away?"

"I don't know," she answered, perturbed she had given little thought to anything other than to get gone. "What bothers me is that I don't feel any guilt. I'm so numb."

Jackie walks over to the fireplace and reached for a book on the mantle. "Thirty days to yourself is exactly what you need."

"Mom, I can't ask you to..." Shannan tried to chime in while keeping her expression neutral.

"Every woman deserves me-time. We spend most of our lives caring for and nurturing others, but how often do we hold space for our wants, needs, and desires? Baby, this book, *30 Days of Me* changed my life. As it reads, "A Kick Start to Your Inner Healing Journey", it's not promising to completely heal you. This author got it right. It's a guide to get you started, but you must have the motivation and will-power to hold yourself accountable the rest of the way. Healing is a forever-journey, Shannan."

"And you're just now giving this to me?"

Jackie let out a weary sigh, but it was tempered with a smile. "You weren't ready then. I'm just happy that you're ready now." Jackie rested her hand on the bottom of Shannan's chin and gently lifted. "Head up buttercup."

"Are you sure this will work for me?" Shannan asked, trying to keep the sobs at bay. "I feel so broken. Sometimes, Mom, I don't know whether I'm coming or going."

"Child, I felt that way too when I left your father," she admitted. "Leaving him meant it would cut me off from the wealthy lifestyle he provided for us. But I also knew that staying would be a detriment to my mental health and well-being. I had to make a choice. I had to either embrace the challenging obstacles that lead to peace or stay on the road to chaos, disrespect, and destruction. That choice was straightforward."

Shannan mulled that over for a moment, realizing that her mother truly understood.

"Mom, I'm just tired. I don't know what to do."

"It took me years to figure it out after I left," Jackie said in a voice above a whisper. "It wasn't until last year, when I came across a post on social media about an author's convention, or something or another. Cavalcade of Authors."

"I've heard of them. I saw them at the Ultimate Women's Expo in Rosemont last year. I wanted to shop, but Zach and the kids were rushing me. Meeting them on that day just wasn't in the cards for me."

"This time, they held an event online. Shannan, it was so much fun." Jackie stroked a hand in Shannan's hair and the move was so comforting she wanted to close her eyes and sleep. "I had never taken part in anything like it. They played fun games with us, gave away books and other prizes, and read excerpts from some of their latest work. That's how I connected to the author of *30 Days of Me*. Jackie let out a long, slow breath. "She read an excerpt from Day 6, a love letter she wrote to herself on her own personal 30-day journey of healing. Talk about heartstrings being pulled—I could see and feel myself in every word she read." Jackie's eyes glazed over with unshed tears. "I had to get a copy. Every day, I committed to reading, doing the assignments and journal entries. When I completed my journey, I felt so much weight lifted off me. I went back online to grab two more copies for you and your sister." This time a tear did fall at the mention of Liz, who had abandoned them the moment Jackie's ex-husband gave her an ultimatum. "Generational relationship curses end here."

Shannan looked up, tears making it nearly impossible to see. "Mom, am I a horrible person for leaving my children this way?"

"You're trying to be a sane person," she replied, lips lifting in a small smile. "And there's nothing wrong with that. It's you-time, Shannan. The babies will be safe with me. The rest of those knuckleheads ... they'll be all right."

CHAPTER 3

Shannan stretched out on the king-size bed in the presidential suite. She closed her eyes, secure in knowing her two youngest children were with her mother and they would be fine. Soon the image shifted to picturing Zach and his brothers at their weekly all-night Monopoly game.

"You've got to be kidding me," Shannan expressed annoyingly to herself. "Leaving just wasn't enough, huh? I still have to witness this mess with my eyes closed?" Shannan picked up the book on the nightstand. Rubbing her fingers across the smooth matte finish, her eyes locked in on the silhouette of the woman with extended arms of freedom on the front cover. She flipped the book to the backside and read:

No one can love you like you can. The best version on yourself awaits you.

"I know that's right," Shannan whispered.

Since we were children, most of us were taught to depend on other people and things for our own happiness, joy, and fulfillment. We relied heavily on acceptance and validation from our parents, caregivers, family members, and friends. Unfortunately, some of us still do today.

In adulthood, often ties our learned co-dependent behaviors manifest imposter syndrome—fueling us with the empty idea that someone or something is needed to make us complete and whole.

Her cell vibrated from an incoming message.

"Speaking of manifesting empty ideas."

WHERE ARE YOU? Zachary texted. WHAT THE HELL ARE YOU DOING?

Shannan needed a moment to process so she got up from the bed and took a seat at her childhood vanity. She couldn't believe her mother had kept it after all these years. She spotted her hairbrush in the top drawer, with her initials S.N.S. engraved in the handle. Shannan admired her reflection as she brushed her dark brown curls. Her focus shifted to the far southeast corner of the room where her twin sister's bed was once situated. The memory of their last argument came to the forefront of her mind.

"Shannan, that better not be my brush." Liz raced over to the vanity and snatched it from Shannan's grip. "E-R-S." Liz shouted angrily. "Mom!"

"It's just a brush, dang."

"It's not just a brush, it's my brush. Can't you read?"

"I left mine in my locker at school."

"What does that have to do with me? That sounds like a personal problem. Maybe if you got up on time when the alarm goes off, you'd have enough time to do your nappy hair."

"Girl, who are you calling nappy? My hair is straighter than yours! And actually, you're the problem. Thanks to dad, you're a spoiled little brat. Between school, band, dance, student council, and cleaning up after you, I'm exhausted—but somebody has to do it. If our list of chores aren't done, then we both get punished regardless of who was supposed to do it. Unlike you, Dad would make me quit everything to do your part, and I'm not giving up anything because you're just plain old lazy."

"Ha, that's cute," Liz countered, giving Shannan a disdainful onceover. "So, you think that stiff body is going to get you a scholarship somewhere?" She followed with a dismissive flick of her wrist. "Oh, I know, maybe you can get a job as a dancing clown at backyard birthday parties."

Jackie burst through the door, "Girls, enough! I can hear you all the way down the hall. What is going on in here?"

Neither one of them bothered to answer. They just went to their corners of the room and sulked.

What Shannan didn't know is that her mother was already dealing with enough. But that day would be memorable for more than just a fight of that brush. Their father laid an ultimatum that separated them far better than a mere argument ever could.

Snapping back into reality she realized she missed her sister so much—arguments and all. What she wouldn't miss is the small slice of peace she'd had just by being away from home for a short period of time. Shannan picked up her phone. No amount of talking before now had produced the long-lasting results she desired. Now she no longer cared. In her mind, her marriage was over. The simple thought of those words was so profound, it lifted a weight from her heart.

I'D LIKE A DIVORCE, she answered. I'M MEETING WITH AN ATTORNEY FIRST THING NEXT WEEK. YOU CAN HAVE EVERYTHING IN THE HOUSE, THE KIDS, THE CAR, THE ACCOUNTS, EVERYTHING. I WANT PEACE OF MIND AND MY FREEDOM.

The text disappeared, and his face and number took up the screen. She swiped an index finger across the glass to reject the call.

WHAT THE HELL? DIVORCE? CALL ME. WHY AREN'T YOU PICKING UP?

BECAUSE I DON'T HAVE TO - she responded - I'M ONLY RESPONDING TO THIS TEXT BECAUSE YOU SENT OVER THIRTY-NINE OF THEM.

ARE YOU WITH ANOTHER MAN?

On that question, she dialed to connect with him. "I barely have time to spread my thighs for you, let alone have time for anyone else. I would've left you long before that happened. I respect my vows."

"Evidently, you don't," he snarled and she could tell that he was barely hanging on to his temper. "It says for better or for worse."

Sprawled on top of the comforter, she focused on the ceiling. "Yes, and it said *or*. All I've been getting for the past few years is the worst part. I'm tired. Just like your mother got tired and found a way to quit. So did I."

"What are you talking about?" he said, sounding as if he'd left the family room for a quieter space.

"Your mother wasn't sick," Shannan said. Her anger—that had dissipated over the last hours—ramped up yet again. "She faked it because she didn't want to do the heavy lifting anymore. Now all she wants to do is pick apart every single thing I do, but takes on none of the work."

"She wouldn't do something that," he said.

"I overheard her talking to someone while she was in the pantry. She said, and I quote—'I had to fake a damn heart attack to get that stupid heifer to get with the program.' Now I'm the one doing the Sunday dinners. Brilliant plan on her part."

Silence, and then, "You're lying," he accused.

Of course, he wouldn't believe her over his mother. "I heard it with my own ears."

"And that's a reason to leave?" he asked, his voice an octave higher than normal.

"I… Am… Tired. I work. I come home. I clean for you. I clean for the children. I clean up after your brothers. You said it's a wife's job, so the boys don't lift a finger and it all falls to me. When your family comes over, they're not supposed to help because they're guests. Seriously? They stopped being guests the minute we said *I do*. They are family."

Zach didn't have a comeback for that.

"Your brothers are lazy and your mother has made them that way. They drop off their laundry at our house, like I'm supposed to serve them as if I'm sleeping with them, too. At least I should get a little pickle tickle out of the deal."

"That's uncalled for," he roared.

"That's keeping it real," she shot back. "I married you. It's understandable that I do things *for you*. They act as if they're paying bills in our household. I thought I was marrying the best man of the tribe. Turns out, even though you're more successful, you're no different from them."

Shannan sat up on the bed. "Have you ever thought about how every time I ask you to stand up for me and you don't—it makes me feel really low, like I don't matter." She grimaced, closing her eyes for a moment to let reality set in. "But I allowed it. I took it—all of it—

much longer than I should. Love does not require that I sacrifice my entire existence for you. I've done enough." She rolled over, pulled out another pillow and placed it behind her back. "I want my freedom. And I'm not playing; not even a little."

"We … we … we can … We can get some counseling or something," he stammered.

"Well, how about that?" she taunted, loosening the belt on her plush white robe. "*Or something.* Because we are way past counseling. When I wanted it, you said Black folks don't do shrinks. I feel you, my brother. Didn't take into consideration that you married a woman who was half White, huh? It's that part of me that's asking for help, but the Black part in me said to get the hell out before I lose what's left of my mind."

She heard his sharp intake of breath and continued with, "So now, let's pass Go, collect $200 and let me pull that Get Out of Jail Free card. Because your brothers and your mother have been on Free Parking and soaking up our life like we're the Community Chest. Now I'm ready to take a Chance and hit the Boardwalk."

"Really?" he yelled. "Trying to end our marriage on a Monopoly analogy?"

"It's all been a game to you. And y'all played it well," she said, sliding off the bed and winding her way through the suite to the window overlooking the Chicago River. "Don't give me any credit for anything of importance. And you weren't like that the first day I showed up for a school that was so different from the private ones I'd known all my life. That was never your deal." Her gaze followed the progression of the Chicago Lady yacht as it sailed toward the mouth of the river that led into Lake Michigan. The yacht, from her view, was so tiny that it resembled one of the metal pieces in that game his family loved so much.

"You know what's funny? You and your brothers play Monopoly six, seven hours at a time every Sunday. I bet none of you know it was originally the brainchild of by a woman—a *woman,* smart enough to create a game that taught the negative effects when something only benefits one person and leaves everyone else lacking."

"That's what this marriage feels like," she confessed. "Lizzie Magie, from right here in Illinois, was intelligent enough to have her shit together. When a man illegally sold it himself, the Parker Brothers came calling. They changed the name from The Landlord's Game to Monopoly trying to steal it out from under her and keep the profit all for themselves." She chuckled. "They still had to come see her because she put in a patent for it twice. A woman did that."

Zach sighed, and she wondered if he'd process the significance of that little known bit of information or brush her off.

"Let me tell you how much the game is like our marriage," she said, pacing the room while figuring a way to bring her point all the way home. "In the original Monopoly, no one was eliminated. Players who couldn't pay their bills were sent to a corner of the board that was called "Poor House"—it eventually became Free Parking. On an emotional level, I'm in the poorhouse. Y'all have been parking all over me for fourteen years ..."

The fact that Zach, the major conversationalist, was silent, spoke volumes. Why did it take leaving for him to shut up and listen?

"Baby, this isn't no kind of right," he said. "You leaving me and the kids like this and you know it."

She laughed again. *She* wasn't being right? "I'm doing things my way this time. I'm doubling my peace of mind. I'll be working towards my own goals. You can have it all. The house, the accounts, Board-walk, Park Place—all of it—even the children. Even as cold as that sounds. That's how much I don't care anymore. You wanted them, now you'll have everything you always desired."

"Except my wife."

"I'm not your wife," she roared. "I am your maid, your cook, someone you sleep with when you feel like it. I've been doing all the giving, everyone else is doing all the taking, including your sorry brothers and Monique's trifling ass. I have nothing else to give."

Minutes ticked by before he responded with, "I still think we should go to counseling."

"And I'm telling you, again, we are way past that," she admitted. "I need to do some things for me. And I can't do any of them being married to you." She inhaled and released her breath slowly. "I can't even lay blame for this at your feet. I take full responsibility for enabling everyone." She paused to take a breath. "Do not call me. Do not text me. I will contact you when *I'm* ready. If you insist, despite the fact that I've asked you not to, I'll turn the phone off altogether. Or I'll let my lawyer handle things."

"What am I supposed to do with the kids?"

"You'll learn just like I did," Shannan said, dragging her fingers through her curls. "You'll be all right."

"You know I'm deeply Catholic," he said. "Divorce is a sin."

"Then looks like we're going straight to hell, because I'm tired of your kind of heaven."

She disconnected the call, finished reading the back matter of her book, and then turned over in the bed. For the first time since she could remember, she had a full night's rest.

Tomorrow would take care of itself.

CHAPTER 4

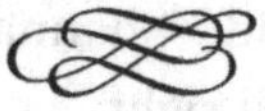

"Mommy, don't leave us here with them. Mommy, please," London pleaded as the FaceTime video kicked on.

Shannan jolted upright in the bed, tossing the novel to the side. "What's going on?"

"They're making me do everything," she said between sniffles. "All the time. By myself."

Shannan was still a little pissed from the text she received from her mother. She put her on notice that Zach had scooped up Kriss and London, claiming he'd bring them back for the weekend.

"It's quiet on that end," Shannan said, shocked by the lack of noise and chatter on a Friday night—only five days after she'd been gone. "Where is everyone?"

"They went to the Bulls game and left me and Kriss here to clean up. He was actually supposed to go to the basketball game, too, but stayed to help me."

Shannan's heart slammed against her chest so hard, taking a breath was hard to manage.

"Mommy, look at this," London said and the live feed switched to the room itself.

Shannan resisted the urge to throw the phone across the suite. The living room and the den looked as though Satan had a wrestling match with his ex-wife and minions, and the minions won.

Clothes, bottles, containers, dishes everywhere. They set the Monopoly game up on the floor, awaiting the players to give it a go. And they were out having a good old time and left her babies to do all the damn work. Oh no, that was not how this was going to happen.

"I had to leave school three times this week because I was going to get in trouble if the house wasn't clean by the time Daddy got home," she said. "I can't do this, Mommy."

Shannan's heart broke. So did her resolve.

"And I'm trying to help," Kriss chimed in. "I couldn't let Lon do this by herself. This is too much for anybody. Even you. And *you're* Wonder Woman."

Shannan's heart melted. Her youngest son's love of comic books was legendary. As was his love for his mother. Being put in the same category as Wonder Woman was huge!

"How long ago did they leave?" she asked.

"About an hour." Kriss said, then pointed behind them. "We got the kitchen straight, though."

"And they're where?"

"The United Center. I think," Kriss replied, scratching his curly hair.

Shannan calculated how much time they would need to gather up things and for her mother to go get them and said, "Pack whatever you can and whatever you think you're going to miss."

"You're not coming home?" London said, her golden face filled with hope.

"I'm sending grandma."

"Yes," Kriss said, pumping his fist. "Storm to the rescue."

Well, Mama does have silver hair.

* * *

"Where do you think you're going?" Zach said, causing London to pull up short so fast that Kriss almost slammed into her. The other five sons filed through the front door and into the living room and spread out, exhausted after a game that had gone until double overtime. The Bulls still lost.

"Grandma's," she squeaked, and her eyes were as wide as saucers. "She's here to get us."

Kriss nodded.

Anger ripped through Zach faster than he could imagine. "Take your little behinds right back upstairs. You're not going anywhere."

"But—"

"Upstairs." He pointed. "Now."

A single tear slid down London's face as she looked at her brother, who took her bag and trudged toward the stairs.

Zach swung the front door open while Jackie still had her fist poised for that first knock. "They're not going with you."

"That wasn't something that was up for debate," Jackie shot back. "They're going to stay with me until all of this is sorted out."

Out of the corner of his eye, he observed London and Kriss tipping back down to the middle point of the stairs.

"You don't get to come here and just take my children from my house," he snapped.

Jackie stepped over the threshold and soon stood only five inches away from Zach. "Did you know London missed three days of school this week?"

Zach's head snapped to London, who cringed.

The older sons filtered out of various points in the house to witness the scene. Zach put a glare on them. "I gave everyone chores, split them so no one person had to do it all."

"Well they," she said, gesturing to Arec, Aaron, Alan, Andres, and Alex. "Didn't get that memo. They left it all to London and Kriss." She placed a hand on her hip, glowering at him. "She left school as soon as she got there to run back here to get things done. Thought her daddy wouldn't love her anymore because she couldn't keep the house clean."

Kriss gripped London's hand as she inched closer to her brother for support. Zach focused a steely gaze on his older sons who didn't seem to be the least bit bothered by the fact that they had unfairly dumped their responsibilities on the babies of the family, much in the same way his own brothers had done growing up. Zach could do nothing right.

Now, he had made his own child feel that way. Made his wife feel that way.

"Go on," he said to London and Kriss.

"I'm sorry, Daddy," London cried. "I just couldn't do it all myself."

Zach stooped so he could look her and Kriss in the eyes. "You shouldn't have to. I love you, baby girl. You too, Short Stack."

"I know, Dad." Kriss puffed out his chest. "Next time, I'll come home with her. We'll do better. I promise."

"No, I'm going to do better," Zach admitted, then watched as Jackie ushered them from the house, but not without giving him a sorrowful glance that served to make a point.

Get your shit together or you're going to be truly sorry.

CHAPTER 5

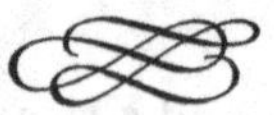

few days later, Zachary Hallerin was so focused on finding the one piece that held his family together that everything else was falling apart. He had to take a leave of absence to learn the budget, where all the money was held, all the arrangements that were in place, handle parent-teacher conferences. He delegated responsibility to each son in an effort to be fair about things. Somehow, he still came home to a house in such disarray he couldn't get a good night's sleep. Dishes and laundry seemed to have married each other and started making porcelain and polyester babies.

Shannan was a magician. That's what it all came down to. He couldn't get a handle on how she managed everything.

"Dad, I gotta be at practice," Arec said, sliding a soccer ball under his arms.

"Okay," Zach said, sighing as reality was back on the main part of his life's menu, making regrets a side order. He leaned over, picking up the clothes off the stairs. "Have fun."

Arec looked at his brothers, then back to Zach. "Um, I don't think you're hearing me."

"I heard you," Zach said.

Alex perched his lanky frame on the edge of the sofa. "Mom takes us."

Zach thought that over, then calculated the one mile it would take for them to get there. "And it's within walking distance."

"Mom drops me off at soccer then takes Andres and Aaron to—"

Aaron's hazel eyes seemed a little panic-stricken. "We're gonna be late."

"Where's London and Kriss?"

"They left about fifteen minutes ago," Alan said, tossing the basketball up, catching it, then tossing it up again before throwing it to Arec.

"Together?"

"Yeah. They've got gymnastics and soccer."

Zach put the laundry basket on the threshold, whipped out his cell and texted his youngest two. They texted back that they were safe. Only then did he breathe a sigh of relief. He faced the rest of his sons.

"Let me get this straight," he said, facing the boys. "The youngest of the crew wanted to be on time and they walked to get there."

"Sounds about right," Aaron said with a shrug and tossed the ball to his right where Andres stood.

Zach thumbed toward the front door. "Get to getting."

Andres missed the ball. "You're not going to—"

"Not happening."

"Man, I wish Mom—"

"You didn't appreciate her when she was here," Zach snapped, and all five of them put their focus on him. "You're part of the reason she walked out."

"Yeah? And you had nothing to do with it?" Aaron said, as his twin nodded. "Why was Mom mowing the lawn? Weren't you supposed to do that?"

Ouch. "She asked one of you."

"Yet, you were in here with your bros while ..." Andres edged, dropping to perch on the stairs. "If you don't, why should we?"

Alex brushed past him, glaring at him on the way to the door. Evidently taking the hint. "Mom's the real MVP in this house."

Now that stings. "Not so much of a champ if she's the only one on the team and everyone else is on the bench."

"Hard to be a team when the coach is outside of the stadium," Alex snapped, then grinned.

"Asking us to do stuff that you're not doing," Andres said, offering Alan his fist for a bump, which he obliged.

Oh, so they could work together when it was to team up against him. "In a minute, you won't have a choice. She's not coming back. And all you'll have is me."

Zach let that sink in for a moment. "And let me tell you this. I played a part in not making sure I did what needed to be done in this house and I'm about to feel the consequences. You all, on the other hand, also chose to ignore the fact she said she needed you." Zach swept a gaze across all five of them. "You all will feel the effects of that, too. Until this house is clean, I'm not shelling out any more money for baseball, football, volleyball, soccer—none of it. Look at this place." He swept a hand to encompass the mess they created daily that was piling up. "I'm the only one trying to do something around here."

"Wait a minute," Andres said, tossing the ball to Aaron. "That's not fair."

"You'll be alright." He shrugged. "I'm going to invite your mother here for a talk. This house—every square inch—needs to be in order."

"What about Lon and Kriss?" Aaron whined.

Zach waggled a finger at all of them. "That little stunt you pulled lets them off the hook."

"Close the door and let's get to work," he said to Arec.

"Now that I'm almost grown, you want to play daddy," Arec taunted, not moving to comply.

"It's never too late to be the father … or the husband I should've been." Zach picked up the laundry basket and slid it to Alan. "I want my wife and my family. Either you can get with the program or you're going to be mighty unhappy around this camp. Your choice."

Alan, Andres, Aaron, Alex, and Arec came to stand at the threshold of the kitchen.

Zach nodded and said, "First, we're going to ..."

* * *

ZACH PICKED Arec up from detention and visited Jackie's home, still trying to track down his wife.

Arec darted up the stairs to be with London and Kriss.

"She's with another man?" he asked Jackie, when she finally allowed him to walk past her into the townhouse.

"I don't think that's the case," she replied, meeting his gaze head on before making her way to the kitchen to finish prepping the meal. Dinner for two. He couldn't remember Shannan mentioning that her mother was dating anyone.

"You expecting someone?" he asked, gesturing to the two wine glasses, two plates, and service for two waiting to be set on the dining room table.

"Nunyo."

"What?"

"Nunyo," she said, smiling. "Short for none of your business."

"Oh, that's cold," he said, chuckling. "I haven't heard that since grammar school."

Jackie put her focus on dicing the scallions.

"I don't understand any of this," he said, settling on a stool at the kitchen island. "I've never mistreated her; never hit her, never—"

Jackie's head whipped up, knife in hand, and leveled at him. "And you're not supposed to," she said, her face a mask of fury. "You don't get brownie points for that." She stabbed the knife in the chopping block. "And that mistreatment thing is up for interpretation. If she felt loved and appreciated, she wouldn't be missing in action. Happy women don't leave happy homes."

Zach never realized how much work it took to run their household. Now, right when things were heating up at work—with Macro Dynamics expecting him to turn in the prototype for a prosthetic for children that was controlled by neuro-cybernetics. The kind of piece that would grow with the children for several years rather than having them outfitted for new ones every few months.

"She's a single woman in a household of seven children," Jackie told him. "If I had to tell you the truth, I would've left your ass a long time ago. She only didn't because she, despite the fact that you let your family roll all over you and her, loooooooooves you." Then Jackie shrugged as she narrowed a gaze at him. "Well, looks like love is no longer enough. Grow a pair or you're going to lose her completely." Jackie nodded in the direction of the front door. "Now get your whiny ass out of my house and get yourself together. Be the man you're supposed to be, not the man that trifling woman is trying to make you into."

CHAPTER 6

$\mathcal{A}$s she pulled up to the Four Seasons Hotel, Shannan allowed the valet to handle her BMW. As she approached the front desk, a smiling receptionist greeted her with,

"Good morning, welcome to Four Seasons. How may I help you?"

"Reservation for Watkins, please. I'm sorry, Smith ... Jackie Smith." Her mother had placed the reservation under her name so she wouldn't have any unwanted guest. Zach was probably calling all of the local venues as she stood there in the lobby.

"Yes, I see it right her. It seems that someone has already taken care of the payment for your presidential suite. Here are your keys."

"Oh, I'll only be needing one."

"Sure," she said, sliding the other one back. "Suite 4600."

The 46th floor? That woman knows I'm afraid of heights. And she had the memories of cleaning her mother's outfit to prove it. They hadn't been to an amusement park since.

"The bellman will bring your luggage right up. Room service is available twenty-four-seven. You can also pick up and dial one to ring the front desk if you ever need anything during your extended stay. It's been a pleasure to serve you, Mrs. Smith. Enjoy your day."

"You as well." Shannan walked toward the elevator trying to keep a graceful glide to her stride. With tears filling the ducts of her freshly mascaraed eyes, she pressed the up arrow embedded into the wall. Seconds later, the doors opened And she took the first step into her unexpected me-journey. A tall, fair-skinned gentleman adorned in a black suit with gold trimmings walked in behind her.

"Beautiful day, isn't it? What floor?"

Shannan was in no mood for small talk. "Forty-six, please. Thank you."

The gentleman exited the elevator on the twentithfloor. The doors closed again, taking Shannan to her destination. She entered her suite and stared, amazed at the beautiful and spacious layout of the room. Since the split with her father and twin, Jackie always made her sure she had the best of the best, from private schools and the latest trendy clothes, but she out-done herself this time. This felt like Heaven.

Shannan made her way toward the living room. She pulled back the curtains, and was pulled in by the mesmerizing lake view. Large bodies of water always brought her peace. But she had to admit that the quiet was a little unsettling. There was never a moment's peace in that house. Always someone needing something, calling her name, in-laws chiming in, marital bed duties to fulfill. Never this kind of quiet at any time.

As she canvased the room, she observed a king bed, two doubles, two marble bathrooms, a powder room, a kitchen, a dining room, a bar, and a small gym. The décor featured smooth fabrics, modern furniture, silk wall coverings, and custom carpets. It was truly remarkable and way more than enough space for just one person.

Shannan tipped back to the living room and stretched out on the gold abstract-shaped couch. She pulled the cell out of the front pocket of her purse and dialed her mother.

"Hello."

"Hey, Mom. This is way too much."

"Oh, I see you've made it," she said with a child-like giggle. "And nothing is too much for my Shannan."

"How are the littles? Are they minding you? If it gets to be too much, mom, I can just..."

"Child, hush." Jackie shot back. "You know I don't play that. We're good over here. You just take this time to focus on you. Don't be calling me every five minutes to check on them, either. I got this. I raised you, remember? Now go on and get started. This journey won't kick-start itself. I love you."

"Yes, ma'am. Kiss the littles for me. Thanks Mom, I love you." Shannan disconnected the call at the same moment a knock on the door startled her.

"Bellman."

"Oh, it's just the bellman," she said under her breath, then raised her voice. "One moment, please."

She opened to find a familiar face. "You again?"

"I...I..." he stammered. "When you saw me in the elevator, I had just arrived for my shift. Here's your luggage, ma'am."

"I'm sorry, I didn't realize you worked here..."

"The name's Franklin," he said, giving her a megawatt smile. "I thought my uniform gave it away."

"Pretty fancy suit for a bellman, Franklin."

"They really take care of the staff here. The guest too. Speaking of, is there anything else I can do for you, ma'am?"

"No, that will be all for now." Then she thought better of it. "Actually, do you know where I can get a good cup of coffee? Sometimes the hotel stuff can be a little basic."

"3 Greens Coffee & Bakery—my favorite place. There's a 900 N. Michigan Mall just outside in the east lot. The place is on the ground level. They have the best lattes around and the staff is friendly. May I ask, are you not from here?"

"Yes, I am. Unfortunately, my busy family life hasn't afforded me much room to enjoy the things I like. Thanks for your help, Franklin."

"Anytime, Mrs..." Franklin looked down at his guest info card. "Smith."

Shannan grinned as she closed the door. She rolled her luggage into the master bedroom, dropped down on the bed, and began unpacking the few items she managed to bring along. Once she finished hanging her clothes in the walk-in closet and putting the toiletries on the marble counter of the master bathroom, Shannan cracked open *30 Days of Me* and quickly flipped to Day 6. She remembered the love letter her mother spoke about and wanted to absorb it for herself:

DEAR ME, *It's nice to finally know you. For so long, you were a stranger to me. I often wondered who you were, but I didn't have the courage to approach you. It was just so much easier to blend in and conform to everything and everyone else around me.*

I've embodied multiple identities, mutating myself into what felt good in that moment. I should have sought you out, but I didn't. I always knew you were amazing, but I often doubted that I could show up for you daily. Instead, I chose lifestyles that neglected my higher-self simply because it was easier.

I allowed you to be manipulated, mentally and emotionally abused while you waited for me; dying for me to stand up for you. I allowed you to be judged and ridiculed. This caused you to be filled with hate, anger, resentment, bitterness, and shallowness.

When you couldn't bare anymore, I watched you disconnect from yourself and from the world. At that time, I felt helpless. I didn't know what to do.

I offer you my sincerest apologies for not fighting for you—for not believing in you and not being there for you. I apologize for not loving you the way you deserve to be loved.

I say to you now ... no more! No more feeling awkward or out of place. No more feeling unworthy. You are valuable. You are limitless. No more feeling ashamed. I accept you for you. No more feeling like you aren't enough. You are and will forever be more than enough. You have every right to be all that you are—and in your image; you are beautiful.

I love you unconditionally. I now put you first. You are my priority. I vow to never lose you again. Coming back from all of what you've been through showcases your resilience. I honor, value, and respect you for that. I promise that you'll never experience anything like it ever again.

I am here to protect you, love you, and care for you. I commit to nurturing you, healing you, and growing with you. I am here to provide you with everything, and I mean everything, that you need. You deserve it.

Love,
Me

SHANNAN COULDN'T FIGHT the waterfall from running down her flushed cheeks and pooling on the robe. She understood why her mom specifically mentioned this chapter. Some parts resonated with her current situation. There were even some things she thought she buried from her past, like the word "no" seemingly being a foreign language to her prom date. First her father, then her prom date, her husband and his brothers, and finally her sons—so much pain and disappointment there.

Day 6 of *30 Days of Me* solidified that this was the right venture for the beginning of her healing journey. Without hesitation, Shannan flipped back to Day 1 to begin her process.

CHAPTER 7

Zach and Arec hit the threshold of Jackie's door. Zach was aiming to find another way to locate Shannan when an all-too-familiar face greeted him at the door.

"Dad? What the hell are you doing here?"

"Unlike you, I actually live here." He sauntered to Jackie and pressed a kiss to her forehead, and she practically melted under his touch.

Zach tried not to let that little piece of information or that kiss knock him off his feet. "Mama's going to kill you."

"Why? I haven't been married to Monique in over twenty years."

"She hates Jackie, and you know it," Zach warned, moving further into the living room where James had made himself quite comfortable —house slippers, plaid robe and everything.

Jackie, Monique, and James had known each other since high school.

"Monique hates everybody," he said, putting his feet up on the ottoman and shrugging. "I know that, too. Makes me no, never mind."

Zach moved further into the room.

"Your mother slept with me that first time—not because she really wanted me, she just didn't want me to be with Jackie," James confessed. "I didn't know that then, but I learned it soon enough when your older brother came along, and she promptly invoked the fact that I was off the market." James grabbed the remote and switched to *ABC News Nightline*, though he kept the sound on mute. "So, she can kick pebbles because rocks are too strong for her." He laced his hands with Jackie's and brought her hand to his lips. "We're grown folks and I don't have to answer to her or you."

"She's the reason you left us," he accused, glaring at Jackie. "You've been tipping around with her all this time."

"I left the minute I could, because I'd had enough," James said, sliding over to make room for Jackie to sit next to him. "Truthfully, I was ready to leave after child number two. Those others were conceived when I was three sheets to the wind. Your mother snuck into the guest room and made sure to extend my prison sentence by extracting a pound of flesh—literally."

Zach grimaced. This conversation quickly devolved beyond his comfort level.

"Things got to a point that I had to stop coming home at night so I could be certain that she wouldn't get pregnant again." James aimed the remote at the screen and switched to *Queen Sugar*. "She was livid and turned all of you against me. I did what was right and fair to all of you. Sent those child support checks like clockwork so you wouldn't suffer from my stupidity."

"She told us we didn't get child support. That you didn't—"

"I have proof. Lots of it. And I made sure to pay through the court, so there was a record and she couldn't keep hauling me in for minor things. They set the amount I paid it and then some."

James kept his focus on Zach, his eyes as clear and devoid of guilt as Zach could remember.

"I don't understand. Where did the money go?"

"Your mother is a career criminal," James explained. He didn't want to share that news. "She used my—actually— your money to open a bookstore and event planning business. Then, to keep it open, she ripped off so many people—hundreds of authors—that it became a class action lawsuit. She couldn't use that money for you or your brothers. She needed it to pay off legal bills. She had good lawyers and lenient judges." He placed a hand on Zach's shoulder. "You boys are the reason she didn't serve any time. The judge was reluctant to put her in jail for forgery, passing bad checks and defrauding people. She has so many mugshots—last count was twenty-two—they stopped putting her pictures next to her arrest records."

Zach dropped on the ottoman, nearly sitting on his father's feet before the man could sweep them out of the way. Now, so many things were clear. They hadn't been poor because their father abandoned them, they'd been on empty because his mother had been draining him and them to cover her own ass. "So why didn't you reach out to us when we got older?"

"Are you kidding me?" James sat up, head tilting to one side as he peered at Zach. "I tried. You all were so much like her. You were too afraid to piss her off and made it clear you wanted nothing to do with me. I respected that, not because I wanted to, but because I had to."

"We're not like her."

"Negro, please." James scoffed, and Jackie averted her gaze as she tried to keep a straight face. "Your mother still has your nuts in a sling. I tried to raise five good men. She preferred to groom five idiots."

"I'm no idiot," he snapped. "I have a career. I have a family."

"About to lose your wife, though," he quipped. "A damn good wife. Not because you want to, but because misery, and you know who I'm talking about, is going to make sure everyone is miserable. Monique ran your brother's wives off so she could have her sons all to herself. And the minute she realized you weren't shaking Shannan loose, she chose another way. Guess where your wife is? On the other side of your marriage bed. And she's going to stay there if you don't get your act together."

Zach felt as if he'd been hit by a sledgehammer.

"Be the smart one in this because there're some things your wife can do that your brothers and your mother can't." James grinned and wiggled an eyebrow. "Try cuddling up next to them to get a little late-night boogie."

"Whoop," Jackie said, nudging James in his side and he gave her a smile.

Arec tipped down the stairs, with London and Kriss right behind him.

"You'd better realize a wife is your companion and not your slave."

"Dad, I messed up so bad. She's not coming back." Zach moved from the ottoman and slumped on the sofa. "She doesn't want counseling or anything. She wants to be free."

"That's what she saying?" James asked with a look at Jackie, who nodded, then shifted her gaze to the silent screen.

"Yes sir, that's exactly what she's saying."

Arec's focus was on his cell between glances at Zach and James.

"That means you've got a bigger fight on your hands," James admitted. "Give her the time she asked for. And work on yourself. You have to change, and not for her." He slid a gaze to Arec, who glared openly at the grandfather he'd never known before today. "Get those little knuckleheads in order, too. All the way in order. They have to know you mean business. Set the stage for you and your wife as a team. That you have everything ready for the captain to return to a tight ship and the lieutenant is on board with the new program."

"Grandma's on the way," Arec announced, getting up from his seat on the stairs. His smile was wider than Lake Michigan.

Zach shifted his gaze to his son, wondering if he'd been dropped on his head or something. "Right, tell us something we don't know."

"I mean my *other* grandmother. Monique." His lips shaped into a smirk that matched his mischievous expression. "You know, the career criminal with all the mug shots. *That* Monique."

"Aw, hell," Zach mumbled, and James tried to hold in a laugh.

Arec's lips drew upward in a face-splitting grin.

Zach resisted the urge to pop him upside the head.

CHAPTER 8

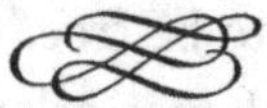

"$\mathcal{N}$othing to be worried about," Jackie said a few minutes later, peering out of her bay window as Monique slid out of the passenger side of Zach's brother, Victor's SUV. She tucked her book under her arm since she planned to re-read and talk about it with Shannan while having a fresh prospective. "I don't know why she's coming, anyway. She's not welcome in my house."

"We just won't let her in," James said with a pointed look at Zach, who nodded.

Arec grinned, then broke away from his father's grasp, ran to the door and unlocked it before anyone could stop him.

Monique Hallerin and her sour expression were over the threshold in the time it took to draw a single breath. "You fat bitch," she snarled, hand snaking out and landing on Jackie's cheek, causing her to reel and stumble back.

Jackie recovered quicker than anyone could imagine. In three swift moves—a right hook, a left jab, and an upper cut—Monique was promptly introduced to the carpet. Face first.

"How the hell are you calling me fat?" Jackie said, leaning down to meet eye to eye with Monique. "When you're two biscuits away from being on *My 600lb Life*."

Monique struggled to get to her feet. She wiped the blood from her upper lip as Zach stood in front of Jackie while Arec ran over to help Monique from the ground. He gave Jackie a wary look and inched backward.

"Been after my husband all these years," she accused, dabbing the blood with her sleeve as she finally made it on her feet. "Low down, no man-having, conniving bi—"

"First of all, he's not your husband," Jackie shot back, motioning for London and Kriss to go back upstairs. They reluctantly complied. She put a hard focus on a grinning Arec and his smile quickly disappeared as he did a Chicago two-step, trying to make it up the stairs before she laid into him too.

"You've been divorced long enough for him to be back on the market several times." Jackie moved in and Zach stiffened, waiting for his mother-in-law to finish what she started. "Second—and this is important, so listen real close. You're in my house, so you don't get to come in here and call me out of my name and keep that one tooth that's actually yours."

Monique moved backward, almost managing that two-step much better than Arec.

"There's an apology in my future," Jackie said through her teeth as though she was barely holding on to her temper. "Whether you give it now or after I stomp a new opening in your ass is entirely up to you." The thought of smacking her across the head with her copy of *30 Days of Me* was tempting, too. Maybe then her peanut size of a brain would absorb some sense. Better yet, hoping the vibrations from the impact would trickle down to that dungeon she calls a heart.

Monique's head snapped to Zach as though he should step in. This fight was a long time coming. He quirked an eyebrow; and though he wanted to move back to give Jackie free range to tap dance on that ass, Monique was still his mother. A mother who had lied to him and his brothers all this time, but his mother was all the same.

Instead, he glared at Monique, waiting for her to comply.

"I'm sorry," Monique said through gritted teeth.

Zach took the stairs two by two, yanked his son by the shirt, and pulled him down the stairs, dragging him to the foyer. "That was messy. I know you called her because there was no reason for her to be here."

Arec shrugged. "Grandma had a right to know."

"Stay out of grown folks' business."

He gave a sly glance over his shoulder at James, then looked back at Zach. "And just so you know, all the bullshit that old man was talking ain't gonna work in our house."

Zach resisted the urge to give Arec the ancestral backhand slap he deserved.

Jackie had no such reservations and went right upside his head. "Ouch."

Zach thought over his son's words for a second, realizing just how far to the left things were with his son. Youngblood had laid down a challenge. Zach needed to make one of his own. "Sure it will. Or I will ship every last one of you little noncompliant Negroes off to military school." Zach grinned, adding, "And watch your language."

That wiped the smile from Arec's face. Now, his oldest son looked worried—as he should be.

Zach leaned in to whisper. "A few months there and you'll be begging to come home. Trust and believe that."

He took in his son's scowl and all the things his father had said clicked. Arec had called his grandmother simply to start the kind of mess that brought people to blows. Since Jackie was packing and her aim was pretty damn good—things could've come to a bullet in the ass; all so Arec could sit back and laugh.

Zach looked at his son, who glared back at him. His two youngest sat next to his father, laughing at some story he was telling.

The changes Zach had in mind meant the people in his family would not be happy campers for a while.

"They'll be alright," he whispered to no one in particular.

CHAPTER 9

When she awakened on the eighth day of her thirty-day hiatus, Shannan finally felt more refreshed than ever. She still had plenty of emotional pain and generational trauma to unpack, but the work she put in felt damn good.

She sat up on the edge of the plush king-sized bed, said a thankful prayer, then slipped out a pair of red silk pajamas and slid into the steaming water of a Nebia shower. With two white bamboo cotton towels—one around her body and one around her curly hair—Shannan checked the weather app on her phone. "Partly sunny and eighty-five degrees. Sundress it is."

She opened the closet door and pulled out a multi-summer colored, striped print maxi dress with a crisscross back. It was everything that it needed to give for the day. The style of the dress mirrored how she felt—flowing and glowing.

Shannan dressed, put on some makeup in the powder room, sat at the office desk and dove back into Day 8 of *30 Days of Me*:

"8 (EIGHT) POWER, authority, abundance, prosperity, wealth, and business

Affirmation of the Day: I have everything I need to be successful.
Theme Song: "Proud of You" by Kalieha

WE'VE all heard the phrase, "You are your own worst enemy". This holds true if you're one of many who are stuck in a scarcity mindset. Operating in your survival mode and playing small makes it harder to go after what you really want in life.

Do you deal with patterns of negative self-talk like, "I'm just not good enough" or "This is too hard, I can't do it?" Are you worried about how you will be perceived by others if you follow your heart and dreams? These are the exact thoughts that hold you back from showing up and achieving your goals. Transform your thoughts and feelings of lack into a positive, abundant mindset.

An abundance block is a mindset block. One of the worst things you can do is not fulfill your dreams, desires, and goals—especially when the reasoning is centered on what other people think about your journey. At the end of the day, it's your journey, not theirs. Your life-destiny was assigned solely to you. It needs no validation from outside sources.

An abundance mindset means to recognize the boundless potential in your life and everything around you. As a result of seeing it, you start believing it. That alone gives you the drive and determination to create the life your heart desires.

Think big, be big, and do big things. Operate day-to-day with a growth mindset. Believe that there's always room to improve and be better than you were yesterday. See your glass as half-full instead of half empty and there's more than enough around you to fill your cup. Perspective is golden.

ACTIVITY: With an abundance mindset, you feel free and find joy in sharing and giving to others. Truth be told, giving is one of the quickest ways to receive. First, cultivate the energy you wish to receive. Then, give it away. By giving freely, you set the intention that there is more where that came from. It'll come back to you tenfold. Today, give some of your time, energy, resources, or money to someone in need.

. . .

JOURNAL ENTRY: Gratitude is the attitude. When you express thanks to the Universe for the things you have and for what's currently working in your favor, you set yourself up to receive more of the same type of energy. Write about all the things, people, and circumstances you're grateful for. Go into detail about how they've made such a positive impact on your life.

SHANNAN GRABBED a pen from the desk drawer and jotted down:

I am grateful for a sound mind and excellent health. I am grateful for my children. They are the blessings that keep me going when I've felt like giving up. I'm grateful for my mother for always being there for me mentally, emotionally, and spiritually. I'm grateful for all the life lessons that brought me to this moment of healing. I am grateful for my husband... Shannan paused on the page, but then continued and the lifestyle he has provided for our family. We've always had a shelter over our head, food to eat, and water to drink. Everything else he has provided for us was a mega-bonus.

Hesitant with her pen again, Shannan closed the book. She questioned whether the material things Zach provided were even worth mentioning. In her mind, that was the bare minimum. He shouldn't get praised for doing what he was supposed to be doing.

To lighten the mood, Shannan ventured off across the east lot to the 900 N. Michigan Mall. As she walked toward the entry door, and with all of the tourist activity flowing around her, what stood out was a woman with short blonde hair sobbing and screaming in her car.

A flashback from her morning read enters her thoughts: "Today, give some of your time, energy, resources, or money to someone in need."

Shannan approached and knocked on the driver-side window of the cream Lexus with black leather interior. "Excuse me, ma'am."

The woman rolled down the window. "I'm sorry, I don't have any money." She rolled the window back up.

"Um, excuse me." Shannan knocked again.

The woman rolled down the window again and yelled, "I said I don't…"

"I don't want your money, ma'am. You just looked like you needed some help."

The woman let out a weary sigh, then inhaled a deep breath. "I'm sorry, it's just been a day. "

"It's all right. I get it. I've dealt with these types of days for twelve years straight, no chaser. Would you like some freshly brewed java? I'm heading in to grab coffee at 3 Greens. Would you like to join me? You look like you could use some company right now."

The woman gripped the steering wheel. "That's the thing. My husband ran off with some hussy ten years younger than me. To make matters worse, when I went to check in at the Four Seasons, they declined every one of my credit cards. That bastard put a freeze on all my accounts so he could spend our money … on her."

"Oh yes, now I see why you were banging on the steering wheel—to keep from going upside his head. That's enough to make anyone lose it. Girl, let's get you some breakfast and coffee. Come on. It's on me. I'm sorry, what's your name?"

The woman wiped the tears from her face as she laughed. "Stacy Parks."

"I'm Shannan."

After they had breakfast and a much-needed girl-talk, the two hit up every store in the mall. They made an entire day of it. Shannan bought Stacy all the essentials she would need to get through the week, including clothes. She then checked Stacy into a one-bedroom suite at the Four Seasons for a week under Shannan's name. That would give her time to figure things out. She also brought an eBook version of *30 Days of Me* so that Stacy could put something uplifting into her mind.

Exhausted from a day of retail therapy, Shannan laid across the bed to finish her journal assignment.:

. . .

I AM grateful to have the means and resources to give to others. I'm grateful for a helping heart. I'm grateful for all things that are in alignment with my highest good and the greater good of others.

CHAPTER 10

The next day—a month into Shannan's defection—Zach scanned the elegant décor of the penthouse hotel suite, taking in the serving tray with the remains of a scrumptious breakfast. It made his stomach grumble in protest at the exceptional home-cooked meals she provided. The setting was for one person and for a moment, relief swept through him. "So, you're going to just live here?"

"How did you even find me?"

"Well, I called just about every hotel in the city for weeks. This hotel was my first call. Something told me to check again yesterday. They confirmed you were here. After showing my ID to the front desk and speaking with the manager, they lead me to room 3606. A blonde-headed woman in a robe who looked nothing like my wife greeted me."

Shannan groaned inwardly. "Oh, Stacy."

"Who?"

"Never mind."

"That woman got a little nervous when I said I was going to call the police because she'd stolen your identity. When the front desk clerk came to straighten things out, she slipped up and said that the woman—you—had another reservation on the books as well. The clerk made me realize you were somewhere else in the hotel and I told them you were missing and the police were searching for you."

So at least Stacy hadn't served me up. She knows the last person I wanted to see was Zach.

Now, are you going to answer my question?" *You can't just live here, Shannan.*

She shook her head. "I'm signing a lease for a three-bedroom apartment in a few days. I saw it last week, along with a few others."

Zach's heart sank. "That's going to be kind of tight," he said, pushing aside the churning in his gut. "You have seven kids."

"Actually, I'm only taking London and Kriss with me. The others are all yours. You and your family have more influence over them than I ever did."

"You would split up our family that way?" he asked, taking a seat on a chair near the window.

"This family has been split a long time," she countered, and her tone was resolute. "It's been y'all against me. They see how you treat me and believe it's acceptable. I want peace, and I'd like to have the children who are most disrespected to have some semblance of a normal life."

Zach, who had been in contact with his father, gaining strength and advice, thought about that for a long while before saying, "What do I need to do?"

"Sign the divorce papers when they arrive." Her eyes were devoid of all the love that made her so beautiful. The woman was so serious, it hurt. "I'll take my name off all the joint credit cards. I don't even want alimony or child support, Just London and Kriss and it'll be fine."

"No, I mean, what do I need to do so there isn't a divorce?"

"Nothing." She crossed one leg over the other, her robe opened to give him a glimpse of her creamy thigh. His mouth nearly watered at the sight. His need for her physically was so profound, the ache almost dropped him to his knees. He missed being with her that way, but he missed the way she believed in him even more.

"Baby, are you sure we can't go to counseling?"

Shannan laughed, and the bitter sound rankled his nerves. "Now that it's too late, you're throwing it out there because it suits you." She stretched out on the sofa, and it took everything inside him not to gather her up in his arms, hold her, and tell her how much he needed her. He'd been so busy trying to become an award-winning inventor —and he was damn close—that he'd let the world's greatest creation slip through his fingers. He was busy helping those born without vital parts, or those who suddenly lost them through some tragic circumstance.

Zach stood before Shannan, with confidence in his stance. "You once said that I was the best thing that ever happened to you."

"I guess I stand corrected." Shannan picked up *30 Days of Me* from the office desk. "As of right now, this book is the best thing that's ever happened to me. I haven't had this kind of peace in years. I want more of this. I don't mind a little hard work, but I do mind being in a relationship that is so one-sided." She sighed, and there was a world of weariness in that sound. "Now I need to slant things in my favor."

"You'd be so cold to leave your other children like that?"

"Don't gaslight me. *Your* children," she corrected. An unfamiliar malice in her tone put him on notice. This right here was a whole new Shannan.

"What?"

"*Your* children. As you remind me from time to time. *Your* sons. *Your* little princess. I was just a womb, a way to get what you wanted. I wanted two children, just two because I knew that's what I could handle and still be able to do what needed to be done for my life."

"It's not my fault that fate conspired against you," he said, then kicked himself because that was as heartless to say, as it had been for him to do. Zach had a bad habit of taking advice from the wrong people regarding keeping his family together. He couldn't fathom his wife leaving him the way his four brothers' significant others had. Lowdown outside opinions, coupled with his ill-fated plan, finally backfired.

"I know. It's my fault for not changing doctors again and again until I found one who would tie my tubes without needing your consent." She leaned back on the sofa, curling her feet up under her. "But that's all done now. I feel like a totally different person. I couldn't remember what smiling felt like. Now I do."

"I'm sorry you feel that way," Zach said and crossing the distance between them. "I'm just going to ask you for one last thing ..."

CHAPTER 11

One more chance. Baby, give me one last chance.

"Let me prove to you I'm not the man who has failed to love you the way you deserve to be loved," Zach implored. "That I can change and be the husband I should've always been. Let me show you how much I need you; how much I love you."

"Be honest," she challenged. "You're just afraid to raise those Nubian Nuggets all by yourself."

Zach smiled and shook his head. "No, I can do that. Took some threats, but I'm getting that under control." He moved in, cupped her face in his hands. "What I don't have is the woman who always believed in me, the woman I believed in." He moved closer so there was no space between them as he whispered, "The woman who made me feel like a million when my own family didn't think I'd be worth fifty cents. The woman I already knew was worth every ounce in solid gold, but somehow, I let others take her shine."

He pressed a kiss to her temple, went to the foyer, snatched open the door and walked out, leaving a swirl of emotions in her heart and mind.

Over the last month, she'd taken a leave of absence from her job. She relaxed with beauty treatments, watched movies, and plays, took up cultural cooking classes, and visited art galleries—journaling every experience in her book. She discovered her new favorite pass-time to be long strolls on the beach. Each day was a clean slate to do whatever she wanted without having to check in with anyone. Jackie was on point to contact her if anything needed attention. Taking time for herself was something she hadn't had the luxury to afford.

Shannan stretched out on the bed, tossing the novel she'd been trying to read to the side. Zach's visit unnerved her, but not for the reasons she believed it would.

She still loved him. Everything inside screamed stop being such a hard-ass and keep loving that man, but she couldn't. Giving in right now meant risking being sucked into the vortex and all the hard work she invested in herself for the past thirty days would be in vain.

Fifteen years ago, Zach had faced his family, disregarding every single one of their objections, and boldly told them he was making Shannan his wife.

"Wow." Vincent shook his head in disbelief. "Must be some mighty good snatch to make you turn on us this way."

Curtis chuckled and nudged Victor in the side. He laughed too, but it was a hollow sound. Monique simply glowered, too puffed up with anger to say anything.

"You never have to wonder if it's what's between her thighs that holds the power." Zach put his focus on Shannan, who smiled at him and laced her hand with his. "It's what's between her ears that's most amazing about her."

One more chance for them to prove they could all work together as a team.

Shannan rolled to the other side of the bed and snatched up the cell from the nightstand. "Mom ... can we talk?"

"Um ... sure baby, hold on," she said, and the huskiness in her tone sent off an alarm.

"I'm sorry, Mom. Did I interrupt something?"

"Nothing but a series of mind-blowing orgasms."

"Good grief, Mom," Shannan screeched, grimacing. "That's entirely too much information."

"Just kidding," Jackie teased. "Trust me, I certainly wouldn't be answering the phone."

Shannan placed a hand over her heart. "But what if I was dying and need your help?"

"Then I'd be there on time for the funeral," Jackie said with a shrug.

"That's cold, Mom," Shannan said, chuckling.

"You were always so dramatic," she countered. "What's the scoop, Daisy Dukes?"

"Zach was here."

"At your suite?" Jackie let loose with a low, throaty chuckle. "Are you about to give me too much information?"

"No, we did nothing like that, though I wanted to." Shannan sighed. "Mom, is it a bad thing that I still love him? I mean, after everything."

"Oh no, sweetheart," Jackie replied. "We can't just turn love off and on like a faucet. The kind of love that you all shared in high school was because you all were better together than you were apart." Jackie's bare feet slapped against the wooden floor, and the sound echoed on Shannan's end. "I think what drives him is fear of losing you like his brothers did with their women, so he locked you in. Now he sees that won't work."

Zach mentioned that one thing that made her shine brightest was that she was so pretty that boys—and teachers—had fallen hard. But to him, her mind, the way she turned a phrase; the way she absorbed books as if breathing them in—her mind was a wonderful thing. Shannan closed her eyes, recalling their hours-long conversations. They would pick apart novels—especially science fiction. **Those** were her favorite. Zach had been a break from the monotony of a life where she had to be perfect.

"He was pissed at me for using Monopoly to express how far down the river our marriage was."

"Pissed how?"

Shannan recapped what she'd said to Zach, and her mother whistled her approval.

"That was deep."

"That's something he instantly understood. He's so focused on winning and beating them, it brings out the worst in him." Shannan held onto that thought for a moment. "I never had the chance to tell him the flip-side. There was another set of rules to play the original game. They called it Prosperity. Everyone had a chance to win—as long as they did it together. That's the game I'm ready to play." She leaned against the cool glass of the bedroom window.

"Then play that game, love," Jackie said. "Play by a fresh set of rules. Work towards your own goals from now on—there's a way to do that and still love him, too. You have to decide what you want and balance it against all else."

"Exactly how am I supposed to do that?"

Jackie raised her right eyebrow. "Child, did you read? Grab your book and turn to page seventeen. Let me know when you got it."

"I got it, Mom."

"Good, now read it out loud."

"Mom."

"Go on," she hedged.

"Believe in what you truly want and feed it positive energy."

But what did she want? Not to be held by or to anyone's standards but her own. Not her father's—who flaunted her beauty to his colleagues and business partners, with an unspoken agreement that she would marry one of their sons, if she'd become the mistress to one of the older men themselves. Awful man!

What would this change mean for her? She'd spent so much of her life pleasing everyone else. Her father. Her twin. Zach. His mother.

She was enjoying this newfound freedom immensely. But she had longed for her family to make her feel complete. She missed her sister so much, and Zach filled that void. To walk out of that door, she pushed that love so far down she didn't think it would see the light of day.

One more chance. Baby, give me one more chance.

Then the truth of everything hit her at once—she was afraid of falling; of failing, of losing. She'd already lost half of her family by embracing and loving her mother, who loved her unconditionally. She wondered if she would give up her mother just to have her sister and father back in her life? No. Their love came with conditions. Her mother's love did not. Zach's love came with conditions and none of them included her.

She'd have to balance all of it with her own needs. Self-care is the best care. She'd need more days like her past 30—spa visits and pampering, her career, trips by herself to the places she always wanted to go that Zach didn't have a desire to see. Most of all, she did not want to spend the majority of her time working for her family. She had more of a desire to work *with* her family.

"Mom, I'm so confused right now. After all of this self-talk, talks with you, and the racing thoughts of my mind, I still don't know what to do."

"That's understandable. When I left your father and took you all with me, it wasn't because I didn't love him anymore. It's because I learned to love myself more. You don't have to spend the time justifying your needs to your husband; make them known, stand by them and let him deal. He'll be alright."

Shannan laughed and said, "Yes, he will. And so will I."

CHAPTER 12

Zach enlisted Jackie's help and sent the children to be with her and become acquainted with their grandfather. Shannan accepted the invitation to visit the house so they could talk. Well, it started as a wonderful discussion on finding balance, rekindling the love lost between them, until …

Shannan burst into tears with her naked body clinging to his. She was trembling within the throes of a release so vicious she almost spoke in three separate languages.

Zach pulled away, instantly concerned. "Wait. Wait. Did you … Did I hurt you?"

"No," she whispered, trying to recover. "It's just …" She shook her head. "It's the first in a long while that I've had an orgasm."

He frowned and peered at her as though she'd grown an extra head. "You always have an orgasm when we make love."

Shannan quickly averted her gaze to the freshly shampooed carpet, then forced herself to look up at him. His expression shifted through three separate emotions in succession—perplexed, shocked, then angry. Finally, his face registered an emotion that nearly stopped her heart. Crestfallen. She should never have told him that. This new "honesty in communication" thing was going to be an issue.

"Even that was for my sake?" he growled before storming from the room.

Shannan snatched the sheet from the bed, rushed to the closet and slipped into a thin robe. She found him in the den, staring out at the garden that somehow managed to thrive in her absence. She waited on the chaise, not too far from him, letting her presence be known without intruding his personal space. He needed a minute to absorb the hard truth of their former sex life.

"I'm sorry. Truly sorry." His features were a mask of pain. "If you still want a divorce. I'll sign the papers and … I'll keep custody of the kids if that's what you want, I—"

"I want my husband," she confessed, moving forward to place a hand on his chest. "I want the man I fell in love with. I want the man who will see he's being used and manipulated by people who only love him when it suits them or because he's an open checkbook." She tilted his chin, lowering his sight to match her eye-level. "I want you to stand up for you; stand up for us. To remember that you love me. Before the children, before anyone else came along, you loved … me."

Zach lifted her hand to press a kiss to her open palm. "Did you know about them? Our parents?"

"Of course I did," she whispered. "They've been married for five years. Your father is a good man who tried to be there for all of you, despite Monique's ugly ways. He didn't hide behind excuses,he got out while the getting was good and now he has a chance at happiness with my mother. The woman he loved before Monique did some under-handed mess to separate them."

Zach's mouth parted, but no words came out.

"Zip your lips, hon. That's not a sexy look." She pressed a kiss to his mouth. "You have tried, really tried, even in the short time I've been back, to break out of that path you've been on all these years," she said, drawing them back to the actual conversation. "I know that's hard. And you're doing it because you love me."

Zach leaned in, kissing her gently. "I haven't been happy for a while and I can't put that on you. Deep down, I knew. I knew, and did things and said things that …"

"So, you know this means cutting ties with your family until we get our thing straight, right?"

He nodded. "I'm down for that. They're grown-ups ..." Then in unison they said, "They'll be alright."

"It's not going to be easy," she said. "The boys are going to give us the hardest time."

"It'll be easy enough for me to put that in check." He snuggled next to her and put his arm about her shoulders. "They can't replace you. I hate it took you leaving me for me to realize that. I won't make that mistake again." Zach stroked her cheek. "Maybe I should have a grading system to kind of check how we're doing."

"No, your mother does that. She criticizes everything and everyone and no one measures up. I'm not going to be that way, woman. Why don't we focus on what you're doing right? We communicate about that and make mention when something can be better."

"That's doable," he said with a smile.

"And speaking of things you're doing right ..."

Zach's throaty chuckle echoed in the den as she straddled him and showed him exactly what she was working with.

CHAPTER 13

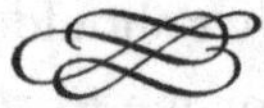

The night Shannan left the suite to come home for a visit, she walked into a spotless house that nearly took her breath away. Zach had worked with her to outline a plan, create a reasonable chore board, spreading out responsibilities so no one person had too much or too little. What amazed her most was that, all by themselves, he and the children transformed the house from that tornado-ridden place to something that looked better than if she had done it herself. Zach even created a cozy office for her to work on her puzzles. This was the best new start she could have ever imagined.

All seven children waited for her in the family room. Even her mother and James were in attendance—a united front, if she'd ever seen one.

"Mom, don't leave us," Arec had said. "We'll do better. Give him—I mean, give us—a chance. Him too."

"Gee, thanks," Zach mumbled, and Shannan stifled a laugh.

"You said we all messed up," Arec continued.

"It's not all on you. We will do better—together." Shannan touched each of their faces, one by one. "I need you. I need your help so we all can be better. I've been so out of it, causing me to lack in being the best mother I can be. I'd like you all to give me another chance to make it work."

"No divorce," Aaron and Andres chorused as Arec nodded vigorously.

Shannan looked at each child before saying, "It's off the table."

Alan sighed, letting out a long, slow breath. "Good. I ... good."

"Family meetings every week," she said. "Thursday, to make major decisions. Dinner every night—together, at the table. I want to know what's going on with you, and for you to talk about things that are important."

That request was met with a range of "cool's" and "that's what's up's."

"And another thing ..." She went to the living room with everyone following on her heels. She held the Monopoly game in the air. "No more of this. You all are going to learn a grown folks' game. A game where you learn to work with partners."

She tossed the board into the waste can and held up a pack of Bumble Bee playing cards. "Spades, then Bid Whist."

"They're not ready," Zach protested.

"Oh yes, they are," Jackie said, chuckling as she snatched up the deck, cracking open the plastic with glee. "You just don't want them to see you get your ass handed to you like you did in high school."

Zach gave her the side eye. "See, why you want to bring up old stuff?"

The children, James and Shannan, laughed.

"Welcome back, Mom," Andres said and led the move for all the children to give her a group hug.

She looked over their shoulders at Zach, who stood smiling nearby.

"It feels good to be home," she said.

Now all they had to do was put her in-laws on notice that there was a new sheriff and deputy in town.

Somehow, Shannan didn't think that would go over so well.

CHAPTER 14

*M*onique and the four Hallerin brothers sailed through the front door like clockwork, filed into the dining room, and froze at the threshold. The dining table had a lovely floral arrangement, but not a single plate or platter of food awaiting them.

"What gives?" Monique said, glaring at Shannan, who met it head on with a bland one of her own.

Zach gestured to the living room. "Have a seat."

They gathered around as Zach shooed the children back upstairs.

"No more Sunday dinners for a while."

That declaration was met with pure silence so thick it could have stopped rush hour traffic.

"So, she's got you by the balls now?" Victor taunted, his mouth curved into a sly smile.

"At least some woman is wrapping her fingers around mine," Zach shot back. "Can you say the same?"

"Oh, that's cold," Curtis mumbled, coming to stand next to his older brother.

"That's truth." Zach put his arm around Shannan's shoulder.

Monique's round face was a mask of unconcealed fury. "You're gonna let that woman separate you from your family?"

"I'm not letting her do anything," Zach replied. "I realize two things. One, she's married to me, not you. Two, she doesn't owe you a damn thing."

His brothers shifted uncomfortably. So did Monique.

"Not dinner. Not a laundry and dry cleaning service. Not for you to lounge around and have her wait on you as if you were her husband. None of that."

As the youngest of the crew, he had never spoken up for himself. He was bullied and pranked so often growing up that giving in was always the safest route to go. But he wasn't that scared little boy anymore. He had a wife, a family, and goals—and none of them would be jeopardized by four men who still had their heads so far up their asses they'd be spitting shit for their rest of their lives. Unless they found out how deep Monique's deception went.

"I'm going to say this… unless any of you can take her place in my life and accomplish what she does daily, then I'm supporting her one hundred percent when it comes to the rules of our house. I'm not losing my wife or my life because y'all are too lazy and foolish to get up and get your own. She is my wife and I'm not going to let you, the kids, or even myself run her into the ground."

"But what about me?" Monique whined, her arms flapping with each movement.

"You have grown sons," Zach explained. "One of them has never moved out because you enable him. That's your right, but do not expect me to put any more money into a household when you have able-bodied men who can take care of themselves and you, too."

She looked from Shannan to Zach. "You just gonna leave me hanging for her?"

"Hanging?" Zach roared. "I have seven children of my own. *They* are my responsibility. Brian and Victor only live with you. Now they can put all of that money to good use—taking care of you, paying your first and second mortgage, and all the things they should've been doing all along." Zach swept a glance from her to each one of his brothers. "You have them. You'll be alright."

"If at any point my wife ever decides to have a dinner and invite you, you all are not guests. You'll be expected to pitch in, bring a dish, wash a dish, clear the table—whatever she sees fit. I have a second chance at love and I'm not letting none of y'all mess things up for me." He looked at his brothers and then told them the rest of what James had shared with him.

"You'll spend the rest of your lives trying to stay under her thumb or you can go out there and get your life. I'm making that effort to let go of anything that doesn't mean me any good. I'm finally feeling like a grown ass man. And it's a good feeling, too. You should try it some time."

Victor, Vincent, Brian and Curtis glared at Monique, who seemed to wither under all the accusations and the unraveling web of lies she had spun all these years.

Shannan walked over to the bookshelf and grabbed a brand-new copy of *30 Days of Me*. "I initially bought this for London, should she ever need it. But she won't. Generational relationship trauma ends with me." Shannan embraced her mother-in-law whose jaw nearly dragged the floor. "I hope reading this and doing the assignments helps you like it helped me."

The children filed down the stairs, spread out to take a seat on them and looked at their father in a signal that more important things awaited. Shannon's cell vibrated and London looked at the screen and said, "It's grandma," then tipped back up the stairs to take the call.

"Now that we've come to an understanding." Zach went to the front door and opened it again, gesturing to the outside with a thumb. "We'll get together at some point, but I'm going to need y'all to step lively. We have a Bid Whist challenge on the table. Me and my wife need to show these youngsters who's boss."

Snickers echoed from the peanut gallery as his brothers and mother finally left. Zach gazed at the seven children looking down at him and then winked.

"Mom, grandma's on the line," London said holding out her cell. "She heard from someone named Liz—Auntie Liz? She's flying in tomorrow and wants to see you."

Shannan's heart filled with so much joy, she leaned into her husband who had a wide smile of his own. She kissed him on the cheek as she said, "Let's get to work."

* * *

THANK you for reading *Sugar Ain't So Sweet*. Please take the time to leave a review.

STOP IN THE NAME OF LOVE

"When did policemen start looking like *that*?" Elise Payne gasped, putting a tighter grip on the steering wheel.

She had been pulled over for speeding but she couldn't believe that someone as breathtaking as Officer Friendly had stepped out of the cruiser. The man had expressive, dark brown eyes and smooth golden features—a proud nose and sensuously curved lips—carved into a ruggedly handsome face that was damn pleasant to look at along with a muscular body that was nothing but pleasure to watch. Elise normally enjoyed milk chocolate, but maybe it was time to give vanilla bean some consideration.

The fact that this delay would probably make her miss the train slipped her mind as she became totally smitten by the most handsome male since Jesus turned water into wine. She could picture those gorgeous lips doing wicked, forbidden things to her—the kind of things that made a woman start speaking in tongues, the kind of things that made a woman leave religion at the altar and dive headfirst into temptation, skinny dip in an overdose of sin, and—

"License, insurance, and registration, ma'am."

Her fantasy circled the bowl and flushed right down the drain with those words. She let out a long, slow breath and said, "May I take my hands off the steering wheel?"

He nodded, grimacing as he did so.

Elise inched her hand into her satchel and produced a license, then leaned toward the glove compartment and froze at the thoughts whipping through her mind. *Registration, no problem. Insurance, huuuuge problem. Expired. Five hundred dollars.*

She tried to keep the despair from showing on her face as she slid the documents to him. Elise watched his every move as he snailed a walk back to his cruiser.

Seriously? Can't you go any faster?!

Several minutes ticked by before he returned. She quickly put her hands on the wheel before he made it all the way to the driver side window.

This time, he sighed with impatience. "It's safe to take your hands off the wheel, Ms. Payne. I'm a Burnham officer. It's the Chicago police who are trigger-happy."

Elise remained completely silent. Maybe if she zipped her lips, he would give her the ticket and let her be on her damn way.

"Do you realize you were going 77 in a 45?" he asked.

"Actually, I thought it was just 65, but 77 it is," she shot back.

He paused for a moment, his right eyebrow lifting. Elise saw a sudden slight uplift at the corners of his lips. There was a fullness that made them the most kissable pair she'd seen in a long time. What was it about this man's lips that invited her to give him a second and third look? What was it about those dark brown eyes that held a sparkle of mischief, but a smidgen of pain behind them? And how was that so easy for her to recognize?

"*Why* were you going so fast?" he asked.

"Because I was trying to catch that train *riiiiight* there," she replied, gesturing to the silver and orange commuter whizzing past them on a black bridge overhead. Her heart sank. All hopes of landing that new position were gone.

"There'll be another one coming along."

The train disappeared from their view, and she returned her focus to him. "Not in enough time to make it downtown for my first day." She slumped in the leather seat and whispered, "And this one had a chance to go permanent."

The officer looked down at her, as though summing things up, summing *her* up. "Well, I'm not going to ticket you for speeding."

Her grateful gaze locked on him.

"Or for the fact that you weren't wearing a seatbelt."

She opened her mouth to protest that she had only slipped it off because he had taken so long, but shut it and nodded her thanks.

"Or for the fact that your insurance expired last week."

"Thank you, Officer Montgomery," she murmured as he slid the items back to her. Their hands touched briefly, and a jolt of electricity whipped through her. She looked up in time to see his shocked expression. *Ah, he felt it too.*

At that moment, however, the only electricity she needed to worry about was ComEd. Her lights and power were about to become a distant memory if she didn't dance into their office with something more than a handful of "give me" and a mouthful of "much obliged."

"This picture," Officer Montgomery said, gesturing to a photo of her with her sister where they both wore black hats--derbies or Dobbs as her grandmother called them. The smiles were from a happier time when they went to a mystery dinner and played detective. They were the only ones to solve the murder that evening and were awarded those special hats by the event hosts. Strangely enough, her ex had been mean enough to take those with him, knowing how much they meant to her.

She explained this to the officer and a sadness came over those dark brown eyes before he tipped his hat. "So sorry to hear that. You have a nice day, ma'am. And leave a little earlier next time."

When he walked back to the cruiser, Elise laid her forehead on the steering wheel. Tears she had been holding back for months finally had their reign. The energy to forge on, to get up and dust herself had never abandoned her—but everything happening at once had finally taken its toll.

Elise moaned as the tears increased. Her entire life was at a standstill and most wasn't of her own making. All of her money was gone. Every single dime she had had been used to keep her twin sister alive, only to lose that beautiful soul to kidney and liver failure last month.

No sooner than she could breathe again without razor blades tearing into her lungs from that loss, did her rich ex-husband swoop down with a team of lawyers and manage to steal her baby boy while she was distracted with grief and the fallout of her family's displeasure at what she'd done to keep her sister alive as long as she could. Yet, she had gathered up whatever resources she could, fought with everything she had, only to lose her son anyway.

Another blow, another setback, another harsh, bitter loss. The last being the one which left her so out of sorts—at least financially. The fact that Ameritech's merger put her and 5,000 other people on the unemployment line was a wakeup call that blared in her ears every day.

Elise sniffled and blindly reached into her satchel for a tissue. She couldn't even drive downtown and park because what she had left in the bank had been shelled out to pay mortgage, a few groceries, and get a train pass to carry her through the month. She didn't complain because at some point, she'd catch her breath and a break—both at the same time.

Fighting for the life of her sister was something Elise would never regret. But the aftermath to her finances and the never-ending strain between her and the family was putting her closer to the edge of emotional bankruptcy.

A tap on the window startled her.

Elise absently patted her tears away with the tissue.

"Ma'am, is everything all right?" Officer Montgomery questioned.

She rolled down the window. "Your kindness was the nicest thing that's happened to me in a long time." She looked up toward the empty bridge. "Thank you. But the next train comes in two hours. By then, the agency will call someone else to take the spot I was going for."

The officer scanned the area. Only a few cars zipped by them. "Traffic isn't bad right now. You could make it downtown in about thirty minutes and still get there on time."

"I could but ..." Elise hesitated then abruptly added, "I can' t ..." She couldn't voice the words—she had everything, down to the last penny budgeted—and parking downtown was an arm, a leg and a couple of someone else's toes.

Officer Montgomery placed a hand over hers. "I'm really sorry."

His touch was wonderful. She centered her self-control with a quickness. "What's done is done. Recently my life has been hit with more curve balls than a dodge ball tournament. So I'm going home to regroup. I'll be fine." Her voice wavered on the last sentence, but she took a deep breath, tossed her hair over her shoulder, and held her head high. Seconds later, she turned the key in the ignition to start the car. "Take care."

Officer Montgomery reached for her hand again. "No, you're not," he ordered. "You will park your car in that lot just ahead. Then you'll get into my car and I'll get you to work on time." He stepped back and finished, "That's what you're going to do."

She looked at him, her tears blurring her vision. "That's what I'm going to do?"

He nodded.

Elise took a moment before whispering, "All right, then."

Officer Montgomery headed for his squad car again and added, "I'll be right behind you."

This time, she did smile ... a little.

Download on Amazon: https://bit.ly/StopinthenameofloveU

Something about him sent a delicious shiver of anticipation up Joy's spine. That shiver did a little curtsy at the base of her neck, before sliding down and sending a tingle between her thighs. Her lips parted of their own accord as if to speak, but no sound would come. The Welcome Circle, where all the rules were laid out for the total strangers embarking on an unforgettable journey, had already started.

"Rule one ... pajamas stay on the whole time," the flaxen-haired host said.

Desperate. The one word centered in Joy's mind followed by a few more. *How desperate did a woman have to be to attend an event simply to experience someone else's non-sexual touch?* She was here, wasn't she? Settled on a sofa in a room filled with people who had come for one purpose—a Cuddle Party, the new wave of safe adult interaction. Everyone played by the same set of rules. The word "no" was met with a comforting phrase, "Thank you for taking care of yourself."

Joy, a single of mother of two, had held onto the article from the *Chicago Red Eye* for nearly a year before deciding to give it a try.

The gentleman had caught Joy's attention as he swept into the room. He removed a large bottle of Southern Comfort from a brown paper bag and set it on the counter as he settled into a spot near the front door. With his back against the wall, he observed the people spread out in several open rooms. The man was stunningly hand-some, with piercing brown eyes, and dark silky hair with a small shock of silver right at the widow's peak. His olive skin had been kissed by the sun, and lips that were the most delectable she'd ever laid eyes on. He wore silk, navy-blue pajamas that complimented his tall, muscular physique. She, along with several others, couldn't help but stare.

"Rule two," their host continued. "You don't have to cuddle with anyone at a cuddle party. Ever."

Oddly enough, Joy expected a place filled with outcasts, people who might have been easily overlooked on the dating scene and everywhere else. Not so. Each man was more handsome than the last. The women were either drop-dead gorgeous or girl-next-door beautiful.

The mysterious stranger remained near the door until it was his turn to share his expectations of the event. The panther-like gait commanded everyone's attention as he sauntered to the center of the living room where everyone was assembled.

"My name is Ali Khan," the smooth, baritone sound beckoned Joy from her thoughts. His voice was as sultry as his appearance, and that was saying something.

The moment his intense gaze met hers, any misgivings she'd felt about being there quickly dissipated.

"I'm here because I love the concept, and the rules. There's a freedom here that's sorely lacking in the world."

As more guests finished their introductions, Joy found that a surprising number of women shared one common thread—molestation, childhood abuse, sexual harassment. Their willingness to share something so personal gave Joy the strength she needed to let her guard down—but only a little.

She glanced at Ali again. One of the rules drifted into the forefront of her mind. *If you mean yes, say "Yes." If you mean no, say "No." If you mean "Maybe," say no. You can always change your mind later.*

Without warning, Ali turned his head and stared at Joy. They were connected across the expanse of the room for several seconds before she broke contact and lowered her eyes. Her pulse raced as if she'd run a marathon mile at top speed, and everything within Joy screamed that if asked, she'd give this man an absolute, "Hell yes."

Chapter 2

She is stunning.

Ali was addicted to pleasure. Nothing satisfied him more than giving a woman the ultimate release, and that was second to the kind that happened between her thighs.

One word described the elegant beauty settled—somewhat uncomfortably—on the sofa. Captivating. The women here, including Joy, were hardly the rejects and low-hanging fruit his sons had warned him about. She had a shapely body hidden underneath a long-sleeve, button-down pajama top with matching pants. The color reminded him of mauve sorbet, and it complimented her honey skin.

Her raven hair hung in loose curls way past her shoulders. Next, Ali focused on her heart-shaped face with full, perfectly kissable lips and expressive, dark eyes that beckoned to him like a trainer waving a steak in front of a hungry lion.

"My name is Joy," she said. The silky timbre of her voice caused several men in the room to shift slightly. He was no exception. "It's taken me an entire year to show up." She lowered her gaze to the pallet positioned on the floor in the center of the room. "And, I'm glad I'm here."

Joy. The quiet beauty and fluid strength were mere enhancements to her appeal. Her eyes were luminous chocolate orbs that held no secrets. She was like an open book to him. He saw the wariness there, then in a flash it was replaced with a glimpse of certainty, followed by an indicator of acceptance. For him? That thought caused a genuine smile to curl on his lips.

Ali welcomed the idea that the rules left no room for doubt. "Maybe" would be voiced as a "No." No quipping, no explanations, no arguments, no persuasion—a simple "No" and the participant moved on with a simple confirming statement. True power lay in the person that respected the other's boundaries. One look at Joy and he became aware that boundaries and walls were relative. He wasn't sure what led him to come this day, but he was glad he'd followed through.

"I'm not sure what to expect ..." He'd heard her say. Neither did he, but the possibilities had become very intriguing.

Ali remained distant, listening to everyone's story. Some with his eyes closed and his heart open. Last year, this approach had garnered a woman whom he had loved and lost. She'd shared a life story filled with such tragedy that his heart hurt every time he thought about what she'd been through. He'd longed to protect her, but through no fault of his own, he had lost her. Family obligation had caused Reign to break his heart. Not because she wanted to, but because she had no choice. He knew all about familial ties. Thankfully, he was on the flip-side of that heartbreak. He wished Reign well and now rejoiced in new possibilities.

Wounded. Betrayed. Strong.

So many vibrations swirled about that woman across the room, but he zeroed in on the two that mattered most. *Survivor. Resilient.*

Those two he could identify with. They echoed in his own life. Ali had never realized he had a "savior complex" until now. Joy had an exotic beauty, and elegance even through the pain that was so clearly etched in her velvet brown eyes. It gave him an overwhelming urge to see her smile.

He thought back to his ready-made life with the built-in wife. Happiness was a constant stranger during that time, thanks to his father. Though he'd understood his father's need to be welcomed back into the family fold, it did little to assuage the bitterness Ali felt at being served up as a physical sacrifice. He'd never wanted the marriage he'd been forced into, nor the burden of carrying his father's penance when he'd married a woman outside of their culture. The sins of the father had indeed been visited on the son.

Ali was a self-made millionaire who had fulfilled all his family's expectations—marriage to a woman from an East Indian family, financial stability, and four children to carry on the Khan name. But that was over. He had no intention of spending the rest of his life in a mediocre marriage he'd never asked for when so many possibilities awaited him. He gained the ire of his father and in-laws when he divorced Sonali, but he had assured them that she would always be financially secure. His duty was done.

Not one for loose ends, in business or his personal life, he had eased Sonali into living a life without him and had no objection when she had run into the arms of the childhood friend.

Now the time had come for Ali to pursue his own happiness, and he had every intention of doing just that.

Dwelling on the past was useless, so he refocused his energy on Joy. No point in trying to hide it. She was the only one he wanted to encounter that night. His mind drifted to thoughts of her lush, sensuous body relaxed in mild supplication, as though the art of seduction seeped from her pores. Her demeanor softened when he introduced himself. That acceptance resonated all over her body as she said the word he'd longed to hear drip from her lips—Yes.

Ali knew then and there—Joy would be his.

Completely.

Chapter 3

"Ali," he said, both snatching her attention away from one of the hosts and startling her at the same time. Joy watched people dispersed into couples and groups, but somehow she'd been oblivious to Ali moving across the room. Now he was mere inches away.

She blinked, trying to clear her thoughts, and inhaled the clean, cool scent of him. So many sensations swirled about Ali that she had a hard time choosing one to hold on to.

"Joy," she replied, extending her hand to him.

"Permission to touch you?"

She hesitated. Oh, shoot. She'd forgotten already. *Rule ... you must ask permission and receive a verbal "Yes" before you touch anyone.*

Complying with the rules meant that every touch, no matter how small, required consent. Permission to touch a hand did not mean the same permission was given to touch an arm.

"Yes," she said in a breathy whisper. "You may touch me."

Ali moved in a little closer. Slowly, he took her small hand in his. Joy noticed the size difference as he stroked a single fingertip across her palm. A strong need hummed within her. It had been suppressed so long that she barely realized the feeling of wanting to be connected to someone. Thanks to her family, Joy was desensitized to any real emotion; starting from the time she'd been forced to leave home at twelve to find a safe place to live.

Don't dwell on the past. Only the now.

Ali moved forward, keeping her hand securely in his. He guided her to the space she'd vacated on the sofa. All around them people claimed chairs, loveseats, mattresses draped in crisp sheets, and comfy-looking pallets on the floor. Guests had also gathered around the kitchen island, holding animated conversations as they sampled an array of food and tempting sweets. The atmosphere was relaxed, but still rife with anticipation.

People of all ethnic groups, backgrounds, and genders were represented, each wanting one thing—to connect. It wasn't surprising that some chose to stave their hunger with food while striking up a conversation before being drawn into any physical contact.

Ali moved closer to Joy. "May I hold you?"

"Yes, you may."

Joy was sitting next to Ali but shifted so that she was now curled into him. The feel of his chest against her face, the muscles that rippled underneath, paled by comparison to his arms securing her in an embrace so wonderful that she did something she never thought possible. Joy let her guard so far down that she suddenly blurted out, "Why are you here?" Only to be floored by his answer.

"I came ... for you."

A jolt of electricity ricocheted through her entire body at his words. Closing her eyes, Joy allowed the safety of his arms to work their magic. The memories she'd held at bay resurfaced, possibly because she was in the safest place possible to relive them. The energy he exuded was that of a man who was strong, powerful, secure in who he was and his place in the world.

I came ... for you.

Those words. He couldn't know what a balm they were to her soul. No one, not her mother, nor her father had ever made her feel this secure. This safe. Not even the family who delighted in treating her like an outcast because she'd refused to follow her mother and sisters into the family business of prostitution. No one had ever come for her. Ever.

* * *

An hour later, the event ended. Reluctantly, Ali stood and helped Joy to her feet.

"I can't tell you the last time I enjoyed an evening so thoroughly."

A huge smile overtook Joy's face. "Me either. I'm so glad I came."

Her happiness mirrored his own. "That makes two of us."

"May I walk you back to your car?"

"Oh, you don't have to," she said dismissively.

"I know, but I'd like to."

A tremor of excitement rippled through her body. "Of course."

Ali placed his hand at the small of Joy's back, and they moved around the room saying their goodbyes and encountered a few genuine smiles, and some that were noticeably forced. It didn't make one bit of difference to Ali.

A touch of humidity caressed them as they left the house. Ali slipped his arm fully around Joy's waist and maneuvered her to the inside as they walked.

"This is me," she said as they reached a silver Buick Encore. She pressed the fob to unlock the door. She slipped inside, turned the car on and lowered the window. "Thank you for an amazing evening."

Ali lowered himself so that he filled the window space. "It was my pleasure. I also had an evening I won't soon forget."

Mesmerized, Joy confessed. "I'm having a hard time leaving because it means I'll never see you again."

He smiled. "There's another Cuddle Party in a week. Meet me there?"

"I'll be there," she promised.

A second later, he released her hand. He gazed into her eyes a final time before he said, "Goodnight, Joy. Be safe and sleep well."

"You too, Ali," she replied.

As Joy pulled away, she glanced at the rearview mirror. He was still standing where she left him.

Download it on Amazon: https://bit.ly/LovingallofMeU

KING OF DURABIA

"You risked your life for my grandson," Sheikh Aayan said, his voice echoing through the ornate throne room. "Ask for anything and I will see what can be done."

Ellena scanned the expectant faces of the throngs of people who had gathered for this unexpected audience with the ruler of Durabia. Most of their tunics and dishdashas differed from her casual attire of a simple white blouse and black slacks. "Thank you, but that isn't necessary. I did what anyone would do."

"Evidently, not everyone," he said, and his angry glare focused on the bodyguard, caregivers, and everyone who had stood by when Javed, the little royal, had swept past Ellena and landed on the moving conveyor belt.

All of them had frozen in place the moment Javed brushed against the rubber bounding strip and was sucked into the void. The video of

Ellena dropping her tote bag, diving in after him, and cradling him in her arms as they were both tossed through the maze of steel and vinyl, all while being battered by suitcases and duffel bags alike, went viral.

Ellena had closed her eyes, bracing under each blow. Javed's laughter was a stark contrast to her pain. The cameras caught everything, including the tail end of the journey when Ellena tumbled out of the final drop onto another belt and finally into the metal cart that would carry the luggage onto the plane. Security finally found their legs and scrambled to make it to Ellena and the little boy before they sustained further injuries. Well, before she did. Her fleshy body was all the protection that Javed needed.

Javed Khan, a great grandson of the Royal Family, was completely unharmed. Ellena, on the day of arrival for a class reunion vacation, had to be rushed to the hospital. They kept her overnight. She sustained a few cuts and bruises that matched the dent in her ego when the entire world saw her tossed head over ass multiple times. And when the adrenaline wore off and the fear kicked in, the little royal refused to let her go. He even had to travel in the emergency transport with her because none of the guards or caregivers managed to force him to release his hold on Ellena.

Now she stood in a palace situated in the heart of a metropolis in the Middle East with a décor that was unrivaled by anything she'd ever seen. Gold—everything was layered with it—the walls, doors, accented by purples and reds that added a sultry warmth to all of the opulence of the furniture, paintings, and draperies covering massive windows.

"Well, to be honest, I haven't wanted much," she said with a nervous laugh. "And the only thing I don't have is a husband. But I'd love to have a place here in Durabia, where I can come and go as I please. If that is at all possible."

"Done," the Sheikh said, beckoning to the man who had visited the hospital twice to see about her condition. "Kamran, come."

"Wait. What?" She laughed and rested a hand on her ample bosom. "An apartment, really?"

"Your new husband," he answered with a grand gesture that would have made Vanna White proud. "This is my oldest son."

The man was drop-dead gorgeous. Olive complexion, dark hair, goatee neatly trimmed to perfection, and piercing brown eyes that missed nothing. He was more suited to a fashion runway than a palace. Truthfully, she wasn't sure if it was the tunics, neat beards, head coverings or what. Durabia seemed to have no shortage of handsome men. But the Sheikh's son was a masterpiece, exuding the kind of confidence that came with a man who was certain of his place in the world. His gaze swept across her face with a complexion slightly darker than his olive tone, then quickly covered the distance over her curves, then his lips lifted in a warm, appreciative smile that practically lit up his dark brown eyes and sent heat straight to places that had been dormant since the Queen of Sheba caused King Solomon to lose his entire mind.

Ellena shook her head, clearing her mind of all manner of wickedness that came after that wonderful assessment. "I think you misunderstood. I was joking about the husband part. The apartment, time share or whatever you call them here, that's all I really want."

"You will have both," the Sheikh commanded with a nod of finality no one would dare to question. "A husband and a place here. My son needs a wife and you mentioned you do not have a husband. Problem solved."

"But doesn't he have to give you heirs or something?" She instinctively brought her hands near her belly. "My eggs are old enough to be married and have children of their own by now."

First, a roar of laughter went up from him. A few moments later, it was mirrored by everyone standing around her. Yes, that line was funny, but the one thing she understood was the unfairness of the situation. At least for Kamran. And that was no laughing matter.

The Sheikh waved away that thought. "That will not be a concern. He is unable to give you or any woman children. And a woman of African descent will never sit on the Durabian throne. We are safe on that score."

A shadow of sadness flickered in Kamran's eyes and his skin

flushed a shade darker. Ellena tried to read a deeper meaning into his father's words. She still came up with *unfair.* "So, you just throw him to a random woman because he can't give you an heir? He is *still* a man. He *still* has value," she insisted. "A brain, intelligence, and a purpose." She inhaled, trying to tamp down on her anger. "The apartment is fine, Sheikh. Thank you, but I will not be foisted on a man who has no say in the matter. That's downright cruel."

A gasp came from the core of people around them before silence descended in the room. Even Kamran flinched.

The Sheikh's face darkened with anger as he slowly came to his feet. "Are you refusing—"

"Give me nine days—"

All eyes focused on the handsome man, who left his father's side and moseyed toward her like some type of Arabian cowboy. All swagger, no gun necessary.

"Give me nine days," he repeated and moved across the expensive Persian carpet until he stood in front of her, towering over her near six-foot height by three inches of his own. "Nine days for me to show you Durabia, to answer any questions you may have. To let you explore the place, the people, the culture. Then you decide."

Ellena found it hard to catch her breath. The man was so virile she felt warm all the way to her follicles. "Nine days? I have to go home. I have a job back there. I used all of my vacation and two of my sick days for this trip."

"Your job?" he asked, frowning as though he couldn't fathom what the word meant.

"Yes. A job. Nine to five. Benefits. All of that. You know, what regular folks do to keep an address."

Kamran remained silent for a few moments as he peered at her. "How much do they pay you?"

She winced, then flickered a gaze to his right and felt the intensity of everyone's attention. "It doesn't matter."

"How much?" He beckoned for her to come nearer. "Whisper it to me."

Ellena hesitated a moment, then complied, moving so close she inhaled the intoxicating scent of sandalwood. She managed to whisper an answer, then inched back to put a little distance between them.

"For the rest of your life?" he asked, his tone and wide eyes reflecting the incredulity registered in his facial expression.

"Until I'm sixty-seven and retire," she replied, daunted by his tone. "But there's also health benefits and other factors that I can't put a number on."

Kamran blinked as though doing a set of mental calculations and coming up with what probably amounted to simple interest on his bank account. "Give me the particulars and I will wire the money into your account."

She parted her lips to protest but he held up a hand. "Saying yes to taking me as your husband is still your choice. With this, I am simply ensuring your peace of mind. And as a gift for your kindness, your selflessness in saving a child who was a stranger to you."

Ellena let out a long, slow breath, because staying here permanently, marrying him, would be a lost cause. She loved her job as a personal assistant at Vantage Point. Alejandro Reyes, a "Fixer" of everything from political and corporate espionage, to terrorist attacks, was the absolute best person to work for. And she loved the predictability of her life. Traveling overseas was the most adventurous event in her life. Still, curiosity won out over common sense and she said, "All right. Thank you."

"Now we go about the business of getting to know one another," he said, smiling as though her consent brought him much pleasure. Evidently, he wanted this to happen and the intensity of his gaze bore into her soul. "So that you can make an informed decision, yes?"

She glanced over his shoulder, taking in some of the envious looks a few of the women tried to hide. "Why are you doing this?" she asked him. "Why are you allowing them to serve you up to some foreign woman as if you do not have value?"

"Because I recognize this is God's will," he answered. "And who am I to leave a precious gift unwrapped?"

Her eyebrows drew in, as she tried to decipher the hidden

meaning behind his words. The man had a peaceful, confident air but also a playful vibe about him.

"Yes, that was a double entendre." His smile widened and she could swear the heavens opened up and smiled with him.

Good Lord, I'm in trouble.

Chapter 2

"You will stay here tonight," the Sheikh commanded. His firm expression dared anyone to question his decision.

"I am here with my classmates." Ellena tore her gaze from Kamran. "We're supposed to see the sights," she protested. "They're probably worried."

"You will be in good hands with Kamran Ali Khan."

"But —"

"Say thank you, Ellena," Kamran whispered, under the Sheikh's fierce frown.

She shifted her gaze to his, saw the warning in his eyes. "Thank you." Then she gave him the Arabic greeting.

The Sheikh flinched, then refocused as he smiled and replied in kind. He slid back onto the throne. "See, she even knows a little Arabic. The proper way to greet. Now your love of Western culture will be put to good use, my son."

"Can he force me to stay here?" she said in Kamran's ear.

"It would be an insult to refuse his hospitality."

"But I don't know any of the customs here—"

"Shhhhh," Kamran whispered, taking her hand in his. "It is fine. You will be fine."

"He can't just throw you away like this," she murmured, searching his eyes for some form of deception. "You don't know me."

Kamran gave her hand a gentle squeeze and guided her to the foyer under the curious gazes of everyone else. "Ellena, nine days is a long time. Today, I will walk you through the palace grounds and then you will give me your original itinerary. I will be certain to take you every place you had planned to see." His dark-brown gaze lasered in on her. "Will that be all right?"

"That sounds nice, but what about the people I was traveling with? This is a class reunion. I haven't seen some of them in ten years. That's the sole purpose of this trip."

"A few inquired at the hospital," Kamran said, walking past the guards at the pathway leading to the exit. "They know you are with the Royal Family. Come, my mother will have a room prepared for you. Tomorrow, we will check into Jumillah."

"What's that?"

"The most precious hotel in Durabia," he said. "And since it is on a private island, it affords the right kind of seclusion."

She nodded, trying to balance herself. All of this was overwhelming.

"Oh, and we are going to the Durabia Mall for you to pick up a few tunics, all right?"

Ellena stopped walking. "What is wrong with …"

"You will be interacting with the Royal Family," he said in a patient tone. "You must cover certain …" He lowered his gaze to the cleavage baring blouse. "*Assets*, accordingly."

She tried to pull away. "It's all too much. It's so fast. What if I make a mistake?"

"You will not. Please do not worry."

Ellena scanned his face again, and could not believe how calm he was, given the circumstances. "Aren't you angry? He just—"

"May I be honest?" he said, and his voice was deep, rich, like the smoothest whiskey.

"Yes. Sure."

"You had me at 'he is still a man. He still has value. A brain, intelligence, and a purpose'."

With that being said, Kamran gave her a slight bow as his mother came forward to guide her into an alcove that led to a suite of rooms. He walked past, leaving Ellena's mind churning in circles.

Chapter 3

"Well, if it isn't our Royal traveler," Dolly teased as Ellena and Kamran made it into the area where her classmates had congregated in the Hyatt's revolving restaurant.

Kamran had called ahead and the front desk informed everyone that breakfast and a meeting would be held around eight. The place had a mix of tables and sofas in green, gold and creams; everything situated so nothing obstructed view of the Durabian skyline.

Accompanying them were Kamran's two bodyguards—Rashid and Waqas, personal assistant, Saqib, along with Saba, the aide they assigned to Ellena to instruct her in palace protocol and to address any needs she might have.

His mother had been more welcoming than Ellena expected, given this culture did not seem to take kindly to interracial marriages.

"My son is a most wonderful, empathic, and enterprising young man," she said. *"Please do not break his heart."*

"That is very premature," Ellena protested. *"He doesn't know me. There's a very good chance I won't hold his heart long enough to break it."*

"You do not know my son," she said with a warm smile. *"He was the one who insisted that you be rewarded for your bravery. And now his reward is a woman who defies his father to defend who he is."* She cupped Ellena's face in her hands. *"You do not know how much that meant to him and me. I have only wanted for his happiness after his father has caused him so much pain."*

"Hey everyone," Ellena said as Kamran whispered something to the guards before closing the distance between them until he was standing next to her.

Damaris, a woman with a warm brown complexion and sharp, angular hairstyle and Dolly, a caramel curvaceous woman, both left their table and came to where Ellena stood. Dolly gave Kamran a lengthy onceover, taking in the white tunic—*dishdasha*—and pants, then his sandals, but she lingered several moments on his face. "Who is this gorgeous man and did they make any more like him?"

"Well, um … he's um …"

"Her royal escort," Kamran supplied with a slight bow.

Kamran's main bodyguard's head whipped around so fast Ellena thought it would fly off. The second one did pretty much the same.

Kamran gave both of them a warning glare to instruct them to stand down.

"Damn, woman," Damaris said with a hearty chuckle. "Leave you in the hospital for one day and you've got a fine ass man on your arm. And you're dressed like the Queen of Sheba."

"Does he have a brother?" Dolly teased, grinning like she was about to hit the lottery.

Kamran simply smiled, put his focus on Ellena and said, "Breakfast anyone?"

"So, it's like that, huh?" Damaris shot back with a sour expression as she wagged her finger at him. "I see what you did there."

"First Tailan gets with that movie star," Dolly said. "Now you're hanging out with the head Durabians in charge."

"Tailan is here?" Ellena asked, craning her neck to find her friend.

"What's that?" Carrie demanded, sidling up next to Damaris and nearly crashing into the woman in her zeal to insert herself in the conversation.

Ellena shrank from her caustic tone and the unwanted interruption. Carrie had been a bully since their high school days. She'd made Ellena's life hell simply because she came from a broken, poor family while Carrie was the result of two high-powered lawyers. Carrie could have attended an upscale private school of her choice. However, her lack of effort landed her in public school. She took every opportunity to remind everyone of how superior her life was to that of every other student.

"On your finger," Carrie gestured to the rock that Kamran had placed on Ellena's hand that morning. His actions were meant to signal to the world that for the time being, she was no longer available for any men to approach her. The minute they hit the Free Zone, an area that was less restrictive, attention was immediately drawn to them. Some of the single male classmates they encountered in the lobby weren't feeling the "message" at all. Several had stepped to Ellena and made their desires known. Right in front of Kamran! Soon, his bodyguards had to run interference before Kamran laid someone flat.

"You weren't wearing that when we got here. So, what's up with that?"

Carrie's voice was loud enough to call everyone's attention to the gift he had personally picked out before they arrived at the Hyatt for breakfast. The jewelry store owner opened the place mega-early just for them. Saba, Ellena's new assistant, was now upstairs retrieving her personal effects from the room she was supposed to share with a classmate. One of Kamran's bodyguards was assigned to look out for Ellena. Being royalty did have its privileges.

"A gift from the king," Kamran answered, his gaze narrowing on the slender woman with a face that had graced a few magazine spreads.

"Wow. What a lucky break." The jealousy in Carrie's green eyes was prevalent. If any doubt existed that she meant anything but, the scowl that marred her pretty face said the rest.

Kamran took Ellena's hand in his and pressed a kiss to the ring, causing her to gasp and a sliver of desire to work its way up and down her body.

"Why did you do that?" Ellena whispered so only he could hear.

"To give her something to be extremely angry about."

"Kamran, you can't claim me like this in front of them," she warned, trying to put a bit of distance between them. Little did he know that his action would bring unwanted curiosity. "People will get the wrong idea."

"Which idea?" he challenged, leveling a heated gaze on her. "That you will belong to me?" His warm smile disarmed whatever nuclear barb she planned to launch his way. "Come, you must be famished."

"Kamran ..."

"Ellena ..." he countered with a megawatt grin. The man was turning on the charm full blast and he knew she was definitely not immune.

Touched that he had picked up on the very thing that would make Carrie so jealous she'd practically explode, Ellena gave him a conspiratorial look. "You are so bad."

"You mean that in a good way, yes?" He wiggled his eyebrows in the most unexpected, comedic fashion and she laughed. "I was thinking that we could have Saba enhance your original itinerary so your group will have a more well-rounded experience."

Her assistant was a bright-eyed Durabian woman that Kamran brought to her room in the palace last night after his mother had settled her in and Kamran returned to take her on that promised tour.

"You mean upgraded?"

He shrugged and didn't make eye contact at first as Ellena avoided the curious glances of her other classmates and their significant others, who were closely watching their interaction. "I am not sure how some of your people will perceive it. I realize you came to explore Durabia with them—and now, I have been added to the equation."

In other words, a compromise was on deck because he wasn't going anywhere.

"They'll get over it," she said. "Let me see what the group organizers have to say." Ellena faced the next table where her friends were chowing down on some of the buffet specialties. "Damaris and Dolly, I need to speak with you for a moment."

They moved away from David, Sheree, Ronnie—all members of the reunion committee, and Dolly put her eyes solely on Kamran. "Sure, what's going on?" Dolly asked.

Kamran explained his thoughts. The two women shared a speaking glance before their faces split in a mile-wide grin. "I'll get a consensus from the group real quick and we can go from there," Damaris said.

Ellena nodded. "Sounds like a plan."

"Yo, listen up!" Damaris bellowed loud enough to cover the distance of the entire restaurant and then some, since their group was the only one present.

Kamran blanched, blinked, and shook his head. Conversations trickled to a halt as everyone's attention settled on Damaris and Dolly who stood near the yogurt station.

"Ellena's royal escort dude wants to upgrade our experience. What say you?"

"What the hell does that mean?" Carrie shot back, voicing the sentiments of the sour-faced crew sitting at the table with her. Former "pretty girls" who hung with Carrie and the men from the football and basketball teams.

"It means we get better accommodations at no additional cost," Dolly replied, her frustration with the homecoming queen—and the fact that half of the people on this reunion trip sided with her for everything—evident. Same way it was in high school. Old habits didn't die hard, they had an afterlife too. "Notice we now have this entire restaurant to ourselves every morning. The buffet wasn't part of our original package, either. You're already benefiting from his hospitality, so quit being all extra."

Dolly stepped forward. "Show of hands. Upgraded with Ellena and the royal dude?"

Half of the hands went up.

"Keep things as they are?" Damaris said in a tone that clearly showed how stupid she thought that choice would be.

The other fifty percent shot their hands in the air.

"All right. It's split." Dolly grimaced before focusing on Kamran "What are we going to do, because I'm rolling with you."

Kamran scanned the faces of everyone. "Those who are … rolling with Ellena, step this way."

Ellena gestured to her assistant to come forward. "Saba, please take their names. Give them to Kamran when you're done."

The woman with a meek demeanor and bright smile, complied and a few people came over to embrace Ellena before she stood aside, allowing them to give their full names and room numbers.

"It is about fifty and two people," Saba said to Kamran when she was done. "With us, and your entourage, that will be a full busload."

Kamran nodded, then to the people around him he asked, "Does everyone have WhatsApp on their cell?"

Some shook their heads, others nodded.

"It will work on the hotel's signal, so I need you to download it right now and add these two numbers," he said before relaying his personal number and also the one to his assistant. "Before we leave the hotel, you will have the new itinerary and any reminders or changes can be sent through to everyone at once."

Saba glided forward and showed him the list as everyone went back to their meals.

Kamran held out his hand and his guard, Rashid, placed a cell in his palm. He then gathered all the current incoming calls into a "group", then typed a single message and sent it to everyone's phone at the same time.

Soon, the persons with the Kamran and Ellena group held their hands in the air, signaling that they received what he sent.

"Hands down," he said. "Our bus will be here directly after breakfast to take everyone to Gold Souk and Spice Souk. We will also visit the Durabia Museum. That will be about sixty minutes from now."

Kamran then whispered something to Saqib that Ellena couldn't quite catch.

"What are you up to?" she asked as his assistant practically skipped away, smiling.

"No good." He lifted an eyebrow playfully in an unexpected manner, causing her to laugh. "I want to make sure the outing is enjoyable for you and your friends."

This man right here. He is playing for keeps.

Download it on Amazon: https://bit.ly/KingofDurabia1
Download it on Kobo: https://bit.ly/KingofDurabiaKB
Download it on Barnes & Noble: https://bit.ly/KingofDurabiaBN
Download it on Apple: https://bit.ly/KingofDurabiaAPC

LOVING ME FOR ME

"With all of those degrees," Devesh Maharaj countered. "I'm sure you're very much aware of the numbers. Black women outnumber Black men nearly three to one. More if you count the ones who are not available to them—married, in jail, gay, or those who don't want to commit to marriage."

The audience clapped, the more enthusiastic applause coming from Black women.

"They'll go to their graves while waiting for the Black man who God's supposed to mysteriously recycle so she can have her turn," Devesh said. "He took two fish and five loaves of bread, and it became enough to feed a multitude. But I never heard of Him using His power of multiplication to create extra brothers when there are already so many other desirable seeds. Those seeds on the ground might at least bloom into a relationship that is more than a placeholder until a good Black man mysteriously comes along. And it might be the best thing that's ever happened for both of them."

This time the audience whooped, hollered, and laughed and Sharon placed an encouraging hand on his shoulder. Sheryl nodded and had an ear-splitting smile.

Shawn's face darkened with anger. "So now you speak for Black women?"

"I don't have to speak for Black women because I only have to focus on one woman." He took a sip from the coffee mug and returned it on the coaster. "A woman I love, a woman whose spirit I'm not going to crush just to satisfy my ego. You have a wife—she's your business. I have my wife—she's my business. I'm not all up in your finances. I'm not all up in your bedroom." From the corner of his eye, Devesh saw Sheryl and Sara nodding and putting the evil eye on Shawn. "Your ego took pleasure in hurting Reign. I take pleasure in helping my woman to heal."

"My woman?" Shawn examined Reign before looking back to Devesh. "Sounds like some cave man white boy mess."

"Number one, I'm not White, I'm East Indian. And my second point is too many men have used the word wife in a way that implies property. Saying my woman is primal, instinctual." Devesh's smile disappeared as his eyes narrowed to slits when they focused on Shawn. "It means I will nail someone's balls to the wall if they come at her the wrong way."

"Are you threatening me? On live television?" Shawn said, shoulders stiffening.

"Not threatening anyone. I'm going to need you to keep my woman's name out of your mouth." Devesh leaned in, causing Shawn to slide back. "See, you're not upset about the most important part of the equation. You're upset about the money. If I wasn't rolling in it right now, you wouldn't blink about who I chose as my mate." Devesh wagged a finger in Shawn's direction. "So my brother, you're going to have to stay mad—I mean the next seventy years worth of mad, because I'm going to be loving my woman until there's no more love to be had."

30 DAYS OF ME

INTRODUCTION

Commencement of the Journey

30 Days of Me started as a virtual self-development bootcamp in November 2020. We were in the dawn of the global Covid-19 pandemic. Many were infected and thousands of lives were lost. Fear, pain, and agony were displayed across all media outlets. My heart was heavy, my mind was clouded, and my emotions were a scattered.

Covid-19 was easily transmitted from one person to the next and was spreading at rapid speed. I often wondered if this was the end of time on earth for all. And if that were true, I knew it was imperative that I center and ground myself. I didn't want to transition from this life with any lingering pain, trauma, or should have-would have-could have's. It was time for a serious deep dive in shadow work.

Just like every other personal growth venture I embark on, my spirit advised me not to go it alone. So before I unplugged from social media and the rest of the world, I made a post inviting other women to join me on a 30-day hiatus.

In total, eleven women answered the call. Most of us were complete strangers to one another but that didn't stop us from being raw, real, and vulnerable right off the bat. Actually, it made it quite easier.

Wasting no time, we began promptly on November 1, 2020. Our intentions we set on self-discovery and recovery. We unpacked the heavy baggage we'd been carrying for days, months, and even years. We cried together, we laughed together, and we most definitely had fun getting to know one another. It was something about women showing up in their most authentic and genuine self that was remarkably beautiful and refreshing. We embraced the ugliest parts of ourselves — and each other — without shame, guilt, or judgment.

Some days were heavy and some were light. On the emotionally and mentally heavier days, we held time and space for one another to express and just be. On the lighter days, we indulged in various artsy activities to unleash our inner child — giving her permission to come out and play.

At end of our 30-day journey, we were met with a sense of relief, peace, and clarity. Even to this day, many of us keep in contact and check in from time to time. A true sisterhood bond was formed. For that, I'm forever grateful.

This process reminded of me the power and strength in numbers. Our vibe attracts our tribe. All we have to do is show up, step up, and speak out. We can go so much further and elevate even higher when we do it together.

It's All in the Numbers

The principles of the work in this book are primarily rooted in numerology. Numerology is the study of numbers and their deeper meanings/connections to life. In this book, you'll be working with the Pythagorean scale to include Cardinal Numbers 1-9 and Master Numbers 11, 22, and 33.

Each number has specific properties/energies associated with it. Recognizing them and flowing with them day-to-day will help you better understand yourself physically and spiritually. If you're dealing with a number greater than a Cardinal Number, but not a Master Number, reduce it by simply adding the digits together to get the collective energy. For example, take the number 12. To get the collective energy, find the sum of 1+2. **3**. The number three harnesses the energies of *creation, creativity, playfulness, youthfulness, joy, communication, and optimism.* When you're dealing with the number three, these are the elements of focus.

Sound complex? Don't get discouraged. I break it all the down for you chapter-by-chapter, day-by-day.

The Best Version of Yourself Awaits You

Like many people, I struggled with the need for validation and people-pleasing. I was my own worst enemy. Unlearning that behavior was no easy task. However, it wasn't until I learned the importance and value of loving and caring for myself that I began to live a happier and freer existence.

Taking care of your own needs and not sacrificing them for the sake of someone else's is essential to your mental, emotional, physical, and spiritual well-being.

Gaining a high regard for your own needs, desires, and happiness will put you in a profound position to set better boundaries, unlock to your inner passions and gifts, and pour your life's devotion into this world.

Enter into a state of appreciation for yourself with this inspirational, transformational self-help book. When you best serve yourself first, you can then best serve others. *You* are who you've been waiting for. Welcome to 30 days of *you* with *30 Days of Me*.

Day 1

1 (one)
Independence, individuality, self, leadership, action, innovation, originality, and new beginnings

Affirmation of the Day:
I choose me. I Am not in competition with anyone except the person I was yesterday.

Theme Song:
"Frequency" by Jhene Aiko

All numbers belong to the Universe, same as everything else in and of this world. How you choose to respond to them and experience them is completely up to you.

One of the most important numbers in Numerology is the number one. Being the root of all opportunities within us and in our lives, it calls you to focus on self in order to achieve your physical and spiritual goals. Everything starts with *you*.

Self-reliance breeds the absence of interference. It's time to start a new phase in your life and accept all the changes that come along with it. You already know what you know. So, release your fear of the unknown and accept the invitation to walk the path of uncharted territory. You'll be surprised at what you can discover about yourself when you surrender to the process.

We are all here with, and for, a greater cause or purpose. Get inquisitive about yourself. Begin asking yourself questions and allow your inner voice to respond. Who am I? What am I? Why am I? Where can I be better? How can I step into who I am destined to become?

Attempt to incorporate 30 days of something else that will benefit your journey. Maybe try 30 days of exercise, 30 days of intermittent fasting, or 30 days of meditation. Consult with your primary care provider before starting any exercise or diet plan. The point is to come up with something else that will aid in catapulting you to your next level during your 30-day journey.

Journal Entry:

In order to invite newness into your life, you first must let the things and people that are no longer serving you die. Start your first journal entry with "I commit to 30 Days of Me. During this 30-day devotion to myself, I release..." Then, make a list of all the things and energies that have been weighing heavily on you. (i.e. fear of judgment, procrastination, need for validation).

Once your release list is complete, make another list to fill the void of what you just emptied. Begin with, "I reclaim my power. I invite back into my space..." (i.e., self-acceptance, progression, or self-confidence).

Purchase your copy today at:
www.authorlaammitai.com

ABOUT NALEIGHNA KAI

Naleighna Kai is the *USA TODAY, Essence®*, and national bestselling and award-winning author of several controversial women's fiction, contemporary fiction, Christian fiction, Romance, Suspense, and Science Fiction novels that plumb the depth of unique love triangles and women's issues. She is also a contributor to a New York Times bestseller, one of AALBC's 100 Top Authors, a member of the Chicago Vocational School Hall of Fame (CVS), Mercedes Benz Mentor Award Nominee, and the E. Lynn Harris Author of Distinction.

In addition to successfully cracking the code of landing a deal for herself and others with a major publishing house, she continues to "pay it forward" with the experience of NK Tribe Called Success, the Kings of the Castle Series, the Knights of the Castle Series, and by organizing the annual Cavalcade of Authors which gives readers intimate access to the most accomplished writing talent today. She resides in Chicago where she is working on her next two books.

ABOUT LA AMMITAI

In a climate where personal development and entrepreneurship is now becoming "The American Dream", La Ammitai is committed to help guide others to their passions, purpose, and fulfill their dreams. La is a highly sought Transformation Strategist & Master Numerologist, who utilizes numerology as the catalyst to leverage personal and professional success. Also specializing in NLP, inner child healing, law of attraction, and manifestation, she has transformed many lives in her unique approach to self-awareness. La believes that everything that one desires is an inside job. Her transparent, action prone approach soars her client's to the best version of themselves. In 2020, La Ammitai lead a group of eleven women on a self-love, self-care, and self-reflection journey titled *30 Days of Me*. The *30 Days of Me* devotional book will be available for purchase in May 2021.

La is a passionate autism activist. Her goal is to shift perspectives and brings awareness to divinely gifted individuals on the spectrum. She is one of the first to discover and openly profess the unveiling of her own innate talents and gifts that she discovered through her autistic children. Through them, she has been able to grapple a deeper understanding of autism and self-reflection through people-connections.

For La, art is love and art is life. She is an artist that uses many mediums as a means of self-expression. La is a gemstone jewelry designer, spoken word artist, vocalist, emcee, motivational speaker and an avid crafter. Her mission is to awaken others to find the artists within themselves.
"Life is a blank canvas. Paint your picture." - La Ammitai

Jewelry and merchandise website: PROTOTYPE ADORNMENTS
https://prototypeadornments.godaddysites.com

Virtual 10K Business Card (all links included)
https://10000cards.com/card/la-ammitai

www.ingramcontent.com/pod-product-compliance
Lightning Source LLC
Chambersburg PA
CBHW010334010826
48970CB00014B/2822